This month's prize:

A FABULOUS SHARP VIEWCAM!

This month, as a special surprise, we're giving away a Sharp ViewCam**, the big-screen camcorder that has revolutionized home videos!

This is the camcorder everyone's talking about! Sharp's
new ViewCam has a big 3"
full-color viewing screen with
180° swivel action that lets
you control everything you
record—and watch it at the
same time! Features include
a remote control (so you can
get into the picture yourself),
8 power zoom, full-range auto
focus, battery pack, recharger and more!

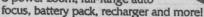

The next page contains two Entry Coupons (as does every book you received this shipment). Complete and return *all* the entry coupons; **the more times you enter, the better your chances of winning!**

Then keep your fingers crossed, because you'll find out by November 15, 1995 if you're the winner!

Remember: The more times you enter, the better your chances of winning!*

PVC KAL

"Look At Me, Nicole."

Obediently, she tipped her head back. The distant glow of the moon's halo glinted from Ace's eyes.

"I'm not hard up."

She had no doubt. He probably had women scattered throughout the world.

"I want you, Nicky, I think you know that."

She nodded, unable to find her voice.

"But I want you warm and willing. You have nothing to fear from me. I'll keep my hands to myself."

"And your thoughts?"

His chuckle was deeply masculine. With bold appraisal, his gaze swept her, lingering on the thrust of her nipples. "My thoughts, darlin'? Well, they're all mine."

Dear Reader,

It's not every month a *New York Times* bestselling writer joins the Desire family, so it's with great excitement that I get to announce that REBECCA BRANDEWYNE has become a part of Silhouette Books. Rebecca's *Wildcat* is not only a very special MAN OF THE MONTH, it's also her first full-length *contemporary* romance. You'll fall in love with rough and rugged oilman Morgan McCain as he spars with spirited Cat Devlin; and you'll never forget their passionate love story!

I'm equally thrilled about the rest of October's lineup. Award winner Cindy Gerard makes her Silhouette Desire debut with the sensuous Western *The Cowboy Takes A Lady*. And if you're a fan of BJ James, don't miss *A Wolf In The Desert*, book #3 in her MEN OF THE BLACK WATCH series.

And if you enjoy time travel—or even if you don't— you'll *love* Cathie Linz's *A Wife in Time*. Cathie's delightful dialogue and sexy stories are, well, *timeless*. Talented author Audra Adams brings us a dramatic story of powerful love and possible betrayal with *The Bachelor's Bride*.

Bringing you a *brand-new*, never-before-published writer is always a special moment for an editor, and I'm *very* enthusiastic about our PREMIERE author Christine Pacheco. Don't miss her first published book, *The Rogue and the Rich Girl*.

Silhouette Desire: we've got something for everyone! So enjoy...

Lucia Macro
Senior Editor

Please address questions and book requests to:
Silhouette Reader Service
U.S.: 3010 Walden Ave., P.O. Box 1325, Buffalo, NY 14269
Canadian: P.O. Box 609, Fort Erie, Ont. L2A 5X3

CHRISTINE PACHECO

THE ROGUE AND THE RICH GIRL

SILHOUETTE *Desire*®
Published by Silhouette Books
America's Publisher of Contemporary Romance

Jared, this one is for you, light of my life, with thanks for the inspiration and unwavering belief.

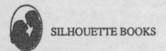 SILHOUETTE BOOKS

ISBN 0-373-05960-4

THE ROGUE AND THE RICH GIRL

Copyright © 1995 by Christine Pacheco

This edition published by arrangement with Harlequin Books S.A.

® and TM are trademarks of Harlequin Books S.A., used under license. Trademarks indicated with ® are registered in the United States Patent and Trademark Office, the Canadian Trade Marks Office and in other countries.

Printed in U.S.A.

CHRISTINE PACHECO

considers herself lucky to have married her real-life hero, Jared. They live in Colorado with their son and daughter.

Christine remembers always wanting to be a writer. She even talked her elementary school librarian into publishing her books. She notes always preferring romances because they're about that special moment when dreams are possible and the future is magical.

Dear Reader,

I don't remember a time when I didn't want to be a writer. Even as a child, I spun fantastical tales, an outlet for a very creative imagination. Along the way, several special people encouraged me in ways I'll never forget.

In elementary school, the librarian actually gave the books I wrote their own shelf and and glued checkout cards on the inside covers. In junior high, a teacher gave me a full year's credit of science projects for writing a book. I can't forget my mother, either, for always encouraging me to believe I could be anything I dreamed.

A lot of things have changed over the years, but not my love of the written word and the power it holds.

The call from Karen Taylor Richman at Silhouette changed my life, helping me realize a lifelong dream.

It's my sincere hope that I can capture your heart and engage your emotions, taking you away to the imaginary world I create. Just for a minute, I want you to take time out of your busy schedule for yourself, relax and enjoy.

All my very best wishes to you,

Christine Pacheco

One

Ace Lawson glanced up from where he crouched on the airplane wing. The taxicab pulled to a halt, and he checked the scarred surface of his watch, not surprised to note it was already ten minutes past the hour.

As the woman opened the back door, he lifted his aviator glasses for a closer look.

Maybe it *had* been worth the wait.

Ankles, then calves emerged. He swore he heard the whisper of silk as she slipped from the car. But that was impossible—the taxi's engine hummed loudly. Obviously it had been too long since he'd been with a woman.

She paid the driver, leaning over to do so.

Ace allowed a long, low whistle.

If only he'd known this was a reward, he would have given up the boardroom five years earlier than he had.

The taxi sped off in a cloud of dust, leaving silence between him and the woman. She walked toward him. With one hand she carried a suitcase, with the other she clutched a tooled leather briefcase. In the wink of the morning sun, he noted the bright red of her sculptured nails.

Auburn hair flirted with her shoulders, a few wisps playing across her face in the desert heat. A skirt clung to her thighs, outlining the length of leg. A blazer hugged her shoulders, thankfully minus any scary linebacker padding.

She exuded professionalism, from her spiked heels to silk blouse. Yet none of the armor hid her obviously dormant sensuality.

Ace jumped from the wing, then leaned back against it, dropping his glasses into place, determined to enjoy the show. He told himself she was a client, that her money paid his bills and bought medical supplies he needed to help the underprivileged. But none of that prevented him from watching the soft sway of her hips.

He allowed a quick grin. Her dress-for-success uniform might look good now, but he'd bet dollars to plane tickets she would be wilted in under an hour. Maybe less. And on Cabo de Bello, where artillery had been flying as often as pesky gulls, the rebels would likely find her an amusing diversion.

Oh well, if she wanted to act as though she were going on the *Love Boat,* he wouldn't stop her.

"Ace Lawson?" she asked, her voice slightly lilting, oddly intoxicating.

"Yep," he said, accepting her outstretched hand. Warm. Smooth. Healthy. A hell of a contradiction to some of the women's hands he'd seen lately. "And you're late," he added. Just like his ex had always been.

"Sorry." Her smile remained firmly in place, although she pulled back her hand.

He wondered if his calluses bothered her. Wondered if the dirt under his nails bothered her. But he'd just finished a run. He wanted a cool shower, a colder beer and a soft pillow, but they were luxuries that had to wait.

"I didn't realize you meant to take off promptly at ten."

He ignored the apology. "Are you going to fly dressed like that? Or do you want five minutes to change?"

"Change?" Her smile vanished and she looked at her sheath-style skirt and spike-heeled leather pumps.

He took in the slick package of her chic appearance. Hell, the lady probably spent more each month on clothes than he'd made in the past ten years. What things he could do for others with that kind of money.

"Honey, you look like a million bucks, but your stockings are going to be glued to your legs and my seats eat stockings for lunch." He shrugged elaborately. "And them heels . . ."

"My heels? What's wrong with them?"

He didn't even try to hide his amusement as she tried to pull the sunken heel from the tar.

"They're stuck," he said unnecessarily.

She grimaced.

He grinned, then rubbed his forefinger across the stubble shading his chin. "Tell you what. I'll give you five minutes to change *into something more comfortable.*"

Nicole Jackson arched a tweezed eyebrow at him. He could well imagine an unfortunate underling receiving that harsh, wordless gesture. It might have terrorized some; it entertained him. "Besides, Cessie here isn't a Learjet."

She cut a glance to the side, taking in the single-engine plane that sported faded paint.

"I noticed."

Her tone irritated him. His Cessna was his only worldly possession, and he loved it as if it were the child he always wanted but never had. Heck, he and Cessie had been around the world several times in the past few years. And she'd never failed him. Unlike the women he'd known.

"So what do you say? You want to take me up on my offer? You're down to four minutes."

She stared at him—nearly eye to eye, he noticed.

"Where do you suggest I change?"

"Over there." He jerked a thumb over his shoulder.

"But that's an outhouse," she protested.

"No attendant on duty, either."

She didn't laugh. Didn't smile. But her brows narrowed into a single, slim line.

"Look," he said, patience waning. "We need to get in the air. If you don't want to change, I'll help you into the plane."

"You'll what?"

"That skirt won't give an inch. You'll have to lift it up or accept my help." Ace hoped she decided not to change.

Indecision warred on her face. Finally, with obvious reluctance, she nodded. "I'll need about ten minutes."

Ace sighed.

"I'll try to cut it short."

She offered a tentative smile and his aggravation began to fade. Then she tried to yank her shoe free.. And failed. With another sigh, he bent, capturing her ankle with his hand. The curve of her bone slid perfectly into the cup of his palm. Suddenly a breath threatened to choke him.

"Really, Mr. Lawson—"

"Ace."

"There's no need to..."

She trailed off as he looked up. Their gazes mingled for a flash of a second. A look, one he hesitated to name, passed between them.

"That is..."

"Yes?" He raised a brow.

"I'd appreciate the help."

"Put your hand on my shoulder," he instructed.

She nodded, setting down her briefcase.

Nothing prepared Ace for the feel of her fingers penetrating his whisper-thin T-shirt. Soft. Warm.

He jerked the reluctant heel from the black ooze, leaving several thin strips of leather behind.

"Thanks," she said, pulling her foot away from his hand.

Pushing to a standing position, Ace watched her slip stocking-clad toes into the ruined pump. Without another word, she picked up her briefcase and headed toward the rest room—outhouse, he mentally amended—once again with that seductive sway.

Hell, maybe this trip wouldn't be so bad after all. For the first time in days, Ace Lawson actually smiled.

Just as quickly, though, his smile disappeared. He had a job to do, then needed to take another hop into Central America.

To kill the minutes, he climbed aboard Cessie and started a second preflight instrument check—anything to keep his mind off what Nicole might look like beneath the tough exterior. Would her undergarments be serviceable cotton, or would they be silk, satin and lace? Did her bra have an underwire or an eighteen-hour support system? Did she even wear a bra?

Ace shook his head. He needed sleep. And a stop at Rosie's in Cartagena. He definitely didn't need a woman reminiscent of his wife.

The heat built inside the small compartment as the California desert sun blasted through the windshield. Hardly a breeze stirred and only a few Joshua trees fought for survival in the hostile environment.

She returned in under ten minutes, white athletic shoes a marked contrast to the black tar. Supple denim snuggled her thighs and hips, conforming to her curves like a good male friend. Or a lover.

His gut tightened.

Ace reached across the cockpit and opened the door. His muscles tightened as he grabbed the briefcase. "What have you got in here?" It was hard to believe she hadn't even struggled under the forty or so pounds.

"Notebook computer, power supply, cellular phone, calculator, modem, files. Why?"

Saying nothing, he reached for her suitcase. The luggage made the briefcase seem light. While she climbed aboard, he secured everything in the small area behind the seats.

Several minutes later, he taxied down the abandoned runway. The plane picked up speed. Out of the corner of his eye, he glanced at the woman next to him.

"Fasten your belt," he instructed, not believing she hadn't thought to do that.

Without checking to see if she'd obeyed, he continued down the rutted, weed-choked runway, easing back on the yoke.

Urging the plane's nose into the air, Ace reveled in the freedom of flight. The engine throbbed steadily beneath him, just like a hot, willing and undemanding woman. The sound of wind rushed past the fuselage, reminding him of the whisper of damp, musky sheets sliding to the floor.

He checked his instruments, then looked at his passenger. She hadn't followed orders. The ends of the safety belt rested at the side of the seat.

Her chest rose and fell in shallow motions and her vivid green eyes stared at nothing, unblinking. The tips of her manicured fingernails dug into her palms, and streaks of artificial color painted her cheeks. Her lips were tightly pursed. Obviously, the grip of fear held her paralyzed.

Ace groaned. He'd been hired to shuttle an uptight businesswoman who got airsick before the land lay even three thousand feet beneath them. "Ms. Jackson?"

A sound emerged from her throat that was part whimper, part moan.

A knot twisted in his gut. The feeling was familiar, but something he'd thought he'd gotten rid of when Elana fled. Evidently not. Unfortunately, he no longer carried a bottle of mint-flavored antacid in his duffel to help tame the wild ulcer. Right now, his passenger could use it every bit as much as he.

"Are you okay?" he asked, hoping he would get the answer he wanted, not the one he feared.

She didn't respond.

A burning in his stomach painfully reminded him of the ulcer's existence.

Taking a hand from the yoke, he frantically dug through the map compartment for an airsick bag. There had to be one. Didn't there?

A bead of sweat trickled down her patrician nose.

"Hang in there," he urged. Ace prided himself on the ability to deal with anything life tossed his way. He'd flown through blazing fires, been shot at, tossed into jail for a crime he hadn't committed, and another he had. And yet, he couldn't deal with something so elemental, so natural.

Or maybe it was the woman herself who unsettled him.

The whimper in her voice became urgent.

"Damn." While keeping one eye on the controls, he reached again and again into the compartment.

She flinched.

And surprisingly, Ace experienced a twinge of sympathy. Digging under the maps, he searched for the waxy-feeling paper. To no avail.

The woman's shoulders drooped, and she squeezed her eyes shut.

Since there were no bags, he had only one option: try to keep her from needing one.

"Open your eyes, Ms. Jackson," he said softly, barely above the lulling hum of the engines. Fighting back impatience, he kept his tone even and cajoling. "You're making matters worse." For both of them.

She blinked.

"Take five deep breaths. Hold each for at least three seconds."

She followed his instructions, drawing in a drink of air. With each breath, his corresponding pain lessened.

"That's it," he added when she gulped again. "Exhale slowly."

She did.

"Now look out the window."

"The window?" The words were hardly above a croak.

"Try and fix your gaze in the distance. Don't look up, and definitely don't look down."

He surveyed the plane's gauges, though in reality he could fly unconsciously... and had done so on more than one occasion.

He noticed her hands had stopped trembling. "Take another couple of breaths, and whatever you do, don't close your eyes, since that makes you more dizzy and disoriented."

A few minutes later, she looked in his direction. A hint of color started to blend with her blusher.

"You okay?"

She nodded weakly. "I think so."

Ace prayed so.

"How did you do that?"

"Learned that handy tip a few years ago. Dated a dancer."

"What does dancing have to do with it?"

"She did ballet—you know all those spins. She said she always tried to focus on an object every time she spun around, said it stopped her from getting dizzy."

"Evidently it works."

"Next time, remember to take your motion sickness pills *before* you get on the plane."

"I did."

He silently pleaded with the sky gods for smooth sailing, sans turbulence. "Are you always such a poor passenger?'' Ace had a hard time believing he wasn't completely irritated by her—with her. Logic said he should have been. She was a painful reminder of his ex-wife and the hurt he'd run—flown—away from. Yet there was something vulnerable about Nicole Jackson, despite the way she dressed and acted. As if there was something more to the picture, something she didn't want anyone to uncover...

Absently he wondered what it would be like to unlock the secrets. Her secrets.

She wiped back a wisp of escaped auburn hair and looked at him. "I do better in bigger aircraft."

Dragged from his wayward thoughts by the sound of her voice, he responded, "Then why do you fly?"

"It's more convenient."

"For who?"

She shifted, squaring her shoulders. He saw her struggle to regain composure, hide the vulnerability he'd witnessed. With her looks, money and title of President, she was obviously accustomed to being in control. Which ought to make things interesting, because he had no intention of relinquishing half an ounce of his control to *any* woman.

"Fasten your belt," he instructed, the words a little rough, as he tried not to notice how alluring she looked with the gleaming sun accenting the highlights in her hair.

Nicole Jackson was business, and in a few days she would be history. Noticing personal things—and wanting to discover them—wouldn't make the trip any easier. And right now he needed easy.

Needed it bad.

* * *

Nicole fingered back the stands of hair that refused to cooperate. Her fingers no longer shook, but an uneasy sensation remained in her stomach. She recognized the feeling, and it had nothing to do with flying and everything to do with being out of control. She detested the feeling, knowing it was a sign of weakness. Nicole didn't want to be out of control, especially when she was at the mercy of a man who didn't appear to have an ounce of mercy in his soul.

To give him credit though, he hadn't turned the plane around and gone back in for a landing. And judging by the expression on his face, the thought had obviously crossed his mind.

Cognizant of his gaze and the fact he'd glanced suggestively, more than once, at the belt, she forced her fingers to relax, then grabbed both ends and snapped them together.

Then he looked away, as if she weren't even there.

While he was deep in thought, or just plain ignoring her, she surveyed the man sitting next to her.

Deep lines were etched beside his haunted gray eyes, indicating that he'd seen more of life than some men twice his age. His dark blond hair was brushed back severely from his furrowed forehead. She knew, without a doubt, that the valleys grooved in his face were formed from experience, not laughter.

A masculine shading of stubble covered his jaw, leaving her to wonder if he'd been up all night or whether the look was typical of his personality. Either way, it was different than what she was accustomed to seeing.

Nicole noticed the way his hands curved around the yoke and remembered the sensual feel of his calluses. The feeling had been unique. And tantalizingly thrilling.

Evidently aware of her less-than-subtle scrutiny, he glanced in her direction. His lips curved into something she thought might be considered a smile in less than polite circles. Momentarily, his harsh features had been transformed, until they weren't quite as brooding. In fact, he was quite attractive. Ruggedly so. Teasingly so. If one went for that type of man, which she definitely didn't. She had enough worries trying to save the account for her client, without adding Ace Lawson to the list of her problems.

"Are you still doing okay?"

Did she detect a slight hint of concern in his tone? "I think you and your plane are both safe."

"Good." There was no mistaking his relief. Nor her own. Obviously, the concern had been a figment of her imagination.

Without another word, he checked a map, glancing at the dials and gauges. He piloted the plane with confidence, almost arrogance. As much as he unsettled her, though, she knew she was in safe hands.

Ace Lawson's firm, Risky Business, specialized in flying people to areas no one else would. She was aware of the recent rebel activity on Cabo de Bello, and knew that was why the last commercial airline had canceled flights to the island. Two months ago, following a hurricane that decimated the runways, the smaller airlines had followed suit. Which left her with Ace Lawson.

Their legs brushed. Worn, nearly threadbare jeans melded to his thighs like a second skin. A jolt of

awareness pierced her. His masculine scent—that of
adventure spiced with danger—surrounded her, making the cockpit intimate.

He grinned wolfishly; he didn't apologize.

She scooted away, pressing her right shoulder against
the cold glass window. She could survive anything for
two days, she told herself. Including Ace Lawson.

After all, she was paying his wages.

And that made him just another employee.

Vaguely she wondered why that thought gave her ab-
solutely no comfort.

Two

Several hours later, a pocket of turbulence jolted the plane. Nicole wanted to squeeze her eyes shut, desperate to keep the consuming panic at bay. But remembering Ace's previous instructions, she forced herself to focus in the distance.

"That's a girl," he said.

She found the deep resonance of his voice oddly reassuring. Nicole clung to the lifeline of his calmness, and decided not to be ruffled by his patronizing manner.

Flying was the worst part of her job. Even though she'd logged nearly one hundred thousand air miles for the company her father started and she fought to save, Nicole had been unable to overcome the constant terror.

And this flight was worse than many of the others. Despite Ace's earlier remarks, she hadn't expected the comfort of a Learjet, but neither had she been pre-pared for the Cessna's cramped confines.

Each sensation was magnified tenfold, from the loudness of the creaking fuselage and constant drone of the engine, to the shudder of the seat and roll of dash instruments.

She hadn't thought she would have to sit so close to the pilot. His muscular thigh, wrapped in faded-to-white denim, pressed against her own, much softer leg. Sensually.

Each time he reached to check an instrument or map, his motions rippled through her. The faint scent of the tropical after-shave clinging to his neck seemed much more potent to her neglected senses than the hundred-dollar-an-ounce cologne she was accustomed to on her male colleagues and rare dates.

He shifted, his hip bone brushing her thigh. She sucked in a huge gulp of air. The man was dangerous, more unnerving than flying, and the aura of power he possessed told her that for the first time ever, she was way out of her league.

Since she'd grown up and learned to deal with the crisscrossing of scars left by an uncomfortable child-hood, that of never fitting in or belonging, never being quite good enough, Nicole had allowed no man close enough to bother her.

And she wouldn't start with Ace Lawson.

Straightening, she inched away from the close con-tact of their bodies.

"I have to stop to refuel before the last stint that'll take us over water."

The unease in Nicole's stomach became acid. Need-ing another dose of Dramamine, she shifted as much as the restricting belt allowed. She grappled behind the seat for her suitcase. When her fingers were unable to locate anything except the coarseness of canvas and layers of maps, she asked, "Where's my suitcase?"

"Under my duffel bag." He turned to her. "You're not sick again, are you?"

"I'm nervous about the landing," she admitted.

"I'll take it easy and steady," he promised.

She wondered if he was only talking about the plane.

"But if you need more medicine right away, there's probably some in the first-aid kit."

She glanced around. "Where's that?"

"My duffel."

The idea of rifling through his personal effects bothered her...more than the thought of the landing. "I'll be okay."

He shrugged. "Suit yourself. But there's no need for heroics. In fact, I'd much prefer you didn't attempt it."

He guided the plane through puffy clouds. Nicole focused on a spot in the distance.

"Almost there."

The plane rocked and bounced as the runway rose to meet them. She gripped the bottom of the seat until numbness froze her hands.

"You can wake up now, Sleeping Beauty."

Nicole emerged from her self-imposed trance like a caterpillar transformed into a butterfly. She blinked, relieved to discover Ace taxiing to the tie-down area.

"You're still alive," he said.

"Tell that to my stomach."

Ace laughed softly, then shook his head. He maneuvered the plane into the spot indicated by an attendant. When he shut down the engine, he turned to Nicole. "You hungry?"

"Couldn't eat a thing."

"You should try something light. This'll be your last opportunity for a decent meal until tonight."

"I'll take my chances."

He lifted a broad shoulder in a hint of a shrug, then dropped it again just as quickly. "We'll be leaving in about fifteen minutes."

Ace swung his long legs to the ground, then came around to her side of the plane. He offered his hand, and she accepted it, surprised by the tingle that chased up her spine at the warmth of his touch.

He released her, moving back a few steps. The motion caused his jacket to flap open. Something metallic glinted in the bright sunlight. She looked again. The handle of a knife.

Nicole gulped. A long knife, the size of the one she carved with at home, was sheathed in a leather holster. Her heart rate jumped. No man she'd ever known owned a knife like that, much less packed it casually on his waist. Instinctively, she knew he had the knowledge to wield it. A shiver of fear traced her spine.

"Is that really necessary?" she asked, her voice betraying her fear.

He followed her gaze. "This?" He pulled the knife from its home with a fluid motion and a vicious hiss.

The sunshine refracted in a hundred different directions, shooting rainbow colors into the sky. The brightness of the glint made her blink several times.

"Yes, it's really necessary."

Pulling her gaze away from the wickedly serrated metal edge, she looked directly into Ace's hooded eyes. He'd certainly drawn the weapon quickly, proving his lazy good looks deceptive. "I received a letter from Governor Rodriguez just a few days ago, saying he was anxious to talk again. He wants this account saved as much as my client does." *As much as I do,* she thought.

"No doubt," he agreed.

His silence, combined with a tense stance, made her push on. In her years as a leader in the corporate world, she'd learned to read body language. And Ace's screamed he was hiding something. "Go on," she encouraged. "If you have something to say, say it."

In a single flip of the wrist, he expertly returned the knife to its worn home. "Look, Ms. Jackson, I have plenty to say about this trip of yours to Cabo de Bello. Regardless of that, my job is to get you there..."

His glance lazily traveled the length of her body. For the second time that day. She refused to shift uncomfortably, but standing still was one of the most difficult things she'd ever done.

When his piercing gaze finally met her face, he was met with her best impression of corporate coolness. But nothing could hide the way her blood rushed through her body.

"...And see that your butt is kept in one piece until I get you back home to your safe, insulated condo in Los Angeles."

"Really, Mr. Lawson—"

"Ace. The name's Ace. We're going to be spending the next couple of days together. You might as well dispense with the formality." Calmly he folded his arms across his chest.

"If that's the way you want to play it..." She allowed her sentence to trail off.

"Honey, I guarantee you, this is anything but a game. The report that crossed your desk last week wasn't a joke. The island's politically unsettled, and I don't mean a comfortable 'vote 'em out of office' mentality.

I'm talking about 'shoot 'em till they shut up' philosophy.''

Back home, in her floor-to-ceiling glass-paned office, the crudely typed report seemed more the stuff of a grade-B movie than her life. Her heart beat faster.

Unfolding his arms, he made one hand into a fist. ''You and your client are trying to change a way of life.''

''Then why did you agree to pilot me?''

''Money.''

Nicole arched a brow. ''Somehow you don't seem the type to require a lot of money.''

''You're right. I don't.''

''Then why?''

''Anyone ever tell you you're a pushy broad?''

''The last man who did wore his front teeth in his lip.''

Ace nearly cracked a smile. Nearly. ''You're welcome to try.''

''I'd prefer a simple answer.''

''Right. I'm taking you to Cabo de Bello because you want to go and I need the cash.''

She waited. And waited.

''That's as simple as it gets,'' he said.

He took her shoulders between his hands, firmly, but not excessively so. That didn't stop a frisson of awareness from passing up her spine.

''I intend to take this opportunity to use every means at my disposal to get you to change your mind about representing your client on this. My beef isn't with you, necessarily, but you're the conduit. And if I take you out of the action, they're out, too.''

Her jaw dropped. She closed her mouth with an audible snap. "You sound as if you have a vested interest, Mr. Lawson."

"Nope." He released her. A warm Pacific breeze toyed with his hair, subtracting years, if not determination, from his face. "I've got friends that don't want to see Cabo de Bello become another sweatshop just to line the deep coffers of your client's purse."

"You're being melodramatic."

"Maybe you're not being realistic," he countered.

"They've invested over four million dollars and two years on this project—"

"Two years is nothing, compared with the way of life you'll change forever," he interrupted, hostility making his words deeper, more husky.

A primitive part of her responded with an internal leap to the sexiness in his voice. Yet, right now, he was on the opposite side of an issue, an issue her survival depended on. "Opening the plant on time hardly compares with ruining a way of life," she said, brows furrowing together.

"Sure it does. Your client..."

She didn't like the emphasis on the last word.

"...Will be getting clothes made at dirt-cheap prices, then selling them for a huge profit. The standard of living won't increase much here, but some fat cat in the States will get even fatter."

"That's free enterprise," she insisted.

"That's robbery. Just because it happens doesn't make it right. Have you stopped to think about the jobs that might be lost at home?

"Be warned, Ms. Jackson," he said, the heat of his breath feathering across her cheek. "I mean it when I say I intend to do everything in my power to send you back with a change of heart. You and your client can find another place that's anxious for your kind of progress."

Nicole shook her head and several strands of her hair met and mingled with his breath. "That's not possible."

More than he knew was at stake. Everything she'd spent years fighting for lay on this deal. If she didn't salvage the project, she would lose the account. God knew she—and WorldNet—couldn't afford it. Because of a series of disastrous failures, her company might be swallowed whole by the highest bidder, maybe by the one person she and her father had trusted implicitly.

Bitterly, she thought of Sam Weeder, her father's partner—her own godfather. Weeder had worked to undermine her company since her father's death. He'd placed a mole inside WorldNet, jeopardizing accounts. Judging by last quarter's financial statements, he'd done a heck of a job.

Failure was unacceptable. She intended to approach success with single-minded determination.

"I can be persuasive." He traced his blunted fingernail down one of her cheekbones.

She winced, not liking the way her treacherous body responded, then pulled back. "I won't be persuaded. Not even if you pull out all the stops."

He grinned. Certain. Cocky. Threatening.

"Fifteen minutes," he said for the second time. "Be ready to fly." Obviously dismissing their conversation—his veiled threat and hinted promise—he pivoted and strode away, long legs gulping the distance to the outbuilding.

Her shoulders sagged against the plane. She hadn't counted on her pilot having an explosive personality,

hadn't counted on the fact she might run into opposition even before she stepped foot on the Central American island near Belize.

Not one to wallow in useless thought, she pulled herself together and decided to freshen up. Standing on her
tiptoes, Nicole reached behind the seat. She bit out a
quick curse when she couldn't shove Ace's duffel off her
bag.

Knowing she could make do with the few cosmetics
in her briefcase, she grabbed it from the floor. Nicole
snapped the latches open and took out a picture of the
plant.

WorldNet's client blended the plant with the island's
natural beauty. They'd spent millions of dollars on the
state-of-the-art plant. It hadn't been until they were
ready to start hiring that the trouble started.

She shook her head.

Saving the account would save her client. And
WorldNet.

Nicole allowed the full-color glossy to flutter back
into place. After digging out the cosmetics bag, she
reached for the box of motion-sickness pills. She shook
out the foil pouch, then sighed when seeing each piece
of foil jaggedly torn. She had another box ... in her
unreachable luggage.

Nicole glanced around for her pilot, but didn't see
him anywhere. And her allotted time was ticking away.
For a few seconds she fought against her conscience,
which told her not to rifle through his belongings, even
though he'd earlier given his permission. Realizing she
had no other options if she was to be prepared when he
dictated, she closed the briefcase, set it on the floor,
then knelt backward on the passenger seat.

She grasped the small zipper tab. The rasp of the zipper sounded unnaturally loud in the summer silence. She groaned when she noticed everything was tightly packed, with no evidence of the first-aid kit. If she wanted the Dramamine, she would have to dig for it.

Inserting her hands down the sides, she discovered nothing but the various textures of fabric—rough and smooth. Trying again, she came across a razor, obviously not used recently, a tube of toothpaste squeezed from the middle and a nearly empty plastic bottle of after-shave. On her third attempt, she grabbed the folded kit. When she pulled it out, a piece of clothing snagged on a torn end of the vinyl.

Nicole tugged on the clothing, suspiciously soft, like satin. She pulled it free, holding it in her hand. "Pinocchio?" she whispered in disbelief. He didn't seem like the type. She pursed her lips. She couldn't believe she'd entrusted her life to a man who carried a knife and wore Pinocchio underwear.

Embarrassed by the intimacy of handling the material that wrapped, probably snugly, around Ace's hips, she gingerly took the nose between her thumb and forefinger and pulled it free from where it had snagged. It was at that second she noticed Pinocchio's nose was designed to accommodate a certain part of Ace's anatomy. With plenty of room for growth.

"Oh my God."

Heat chased up her cheeks. As if they'd singed her fingers, she threw the briefs back into the duffel bag, yanking the zipper shut. The man was too much.

Pulling her professional demeanor around her as a protective barrier, she raided the first-aid kit, leaving it on the seat between them.

She climbed down the plane and hurried to the rest room. By the time she had resculptured her cheek-bones with an artful sweep of blush and pulled her hair back into a chignon, she was in control. Unshakable.

Even by Ace and his less-than-civilized tendencies.

He'd kept her off kilter so far, but she could handle it. Except for the missing polish on his veneer—the crude language, unshaven chin and well-worn blue jeans—he was exactly the same as every man she'd ever met.

An unfamiliar nagging voice reminded her of the long silky nose that had hung between her fingers, Pinocchio's ridiculous eyes wide with delight and mouth smiling devilishly. Of the two men she'd been involved with, one had worn baggy boxer shorts and the other had worn white briefs with standard apples and grapes on the tag. No, Ace wasn't like *any* man she'd known.

Nicole squared her shoulders and left the bathroom feeling confident and composed. Ace was signing the bottom of a fuel invoice when she reached the plane.

He handed the attendant the clipboard, then flicked his gaze over her. "I liked your hair the way it was."

She fingered the secured knot. "I prefer it up."

"Yeah." He took mirrored aviator shades from the breast pocket of his ragged denim jacket. "You would."

She felt a moment of regret when he put on the glasses, blocking out the intensity etched in his gray eyes. Simultaneously, she was glad. He saw too much.

"Ready?"

"Anytime you are," she answered, shoving aside the unwelcome thoughts of his all-knowing eyes. Nicole opened the passenger door and saw a half-dozen or so airsick bags on her seat. She didn't know whether he was being courteous or cautious. Cautious, she decided, moving them to the map compartment. Ace wouldn't have done anything for her comfort, only his.

After a Learjet cleared, Ace taxied into position on the runway, and opened the throttle, giving the engine full power.

She wasn't sure why, but this takeoff didn't traumatize her as much as the first one had. Ace nudged the nose into the air, then leveled off, and her stomach only twisted with sporadic pains. She marveled at the sensation and told herself it had nothing to do with the pilot's obvious skills.

Many hours later, following another brief landing for fuel at a scary-looking airstrip near a small Mexican village, the sun splashed its majestic array of colors across a vivid blue backdrop, then dropped on the western horizon.

She craned her head to look out the window, seeing the world in a new way. Invariably, on commercial flights, she lowered the window shade so she wouldn't be forced to accept the reality of flirting with clouds while the land beneath her melded into a solid mass of potential crash sites.

Magenta swirled with purples and mauves, and she realized it was the first time she'd seen a sunset in over two years. Her job, first as Daddy's assistant, now as sole owner, consumed every available hour and even a few that weren't available. "It's beautiful up here," she said, nearly ten minutes later, after the sun had given a final wink, casting sparkling shimmers into the Caribbean.

"There's no place like the sky," he agreed over the engine's roar.

For a moment, the grooves around his eyes relaxed, and Nicole glimpsed the real human being buried beneath layers of hard exterior. Was it possible . . . ?

Instantly the softening disappeared.

The next few hours passed in a blur to her.

"We'll be landing soon."

Butterflies leapt to life, bringing her out of her silent plans for the meeting with the governor.

"You might want to take some more Dramamine."

"I've already taken some."

"You got them out of the bag?"

She wrinkled her nose. "I met Pinocchio."

"Pinocchio?" he echoed, seemingly confused.

"The underwear in your bag."

Ace laughed, and the sound was every bit as rich and vibrant as she'd thought. Like Kahlúa and cream splashed over big chunky ice cubes. And every bit as potent.

"They were a gag gift," he said. "At the bachelor party I went to a couple of days ago."

"I could hardly care what you dress in, Mr. Lawson." Still, she couldn't help but wonder how they would look on him.

"I assure you, Ms. Jackson, I've never worn anything like that."

She resisted the implied invitation to ask what he did wear.

"Not my style."

Nicole turned away, looking out the window, seeing nothing except the vastness of water, which she assumed was the Caribbean. "I thought you said we're landing."

"We are."

"Where?" she asked.

"Down there."

"Down where?" she asked again, not seeing anything resembling an island, let alone a runway.

Outrageously, he winked at her. "Trust me."

Her stomach dropped when Ace began the descent. Trusting him was the last thing she wanted to do. And the one thing she had to stake her life on.

The plane hit a patch of rough air, causing them to lose altitude drastically.

"We'll be okay."

She clutched the metal bar under her seat, the words *trust me* echoing in her mind.

They emerged from the turbulence, less than a heartbeat later.

"That wasn't too bad, was it?"

"Terrifying," she said.

"That wasn't terrifying," he said. "Terrifying is when you're in the air with a bullet hole in the windshield and a fire in the engine."

His tone was matter-of-fact, and it lit a responding flame somewhere inside her. He'd experienced the danger of living on the edge but didn't allow it to bother him.

"Are you ever afraid?"

Ten, maybe fifteen seconds passed and she thought he didn't intend to answer. What was going on behind that smoky gaze? What was he hiding?

Finally he admitted, "Sometimes. Sometimes I'm afraid."

He looked at her. He obviously had a human side he didn't want to show often. For some reason, the fact that he'd afforded her a glimpse of his fallible humanity touched her.

"Why do you put yourself in a position like that in the first place?"

"Because life can be shallow and meaningless."

He specialized in taking people where no one else would. It had earned him a reputation she'd been scared to trust. Until she'd had no other options. "Putting yourself in danger makes life meaningful?"

"*Living* makes life meaningful," he said.

She started to ask another question, to dig a little deeper into the character he wanted shrouded, but he interrupted.

"The runway's just ahead."

Nicole looked out the windshield, seeing something that resembled a lump of coal, floating in the middle of the sea. "Cabo de Bello?"

He looked at his console again. "Yep."

A single light reflected in the distance. She felt like Columbus, discovering the blessed sight of land after months at sea.

Ace maneuvered the plane into a descent. Of all the things that could happen, gravity concerned her most.

"Hang on," he said. "This runway's still screwed up from the last tropical storm."

She knew that, but hearing him say it made it more immediate. Alarming.

As they got closer, it appeared palm tree fronds grabbed at them like demonic fingers. She swallowed a terrified scream. The landing gear snagged in a rut, making them career wildly. Ace swore. Nicole prayed. The plane rocked and shuddered, and the seat belt sliced across her middle.

"We'll be okay in half a second," he shouted.

The acrid stench of smoking rubber burned her nose. But before she knew it, they slid to a gradual stop, several dozen yards away from a threatening stand of tropical trees.

He'd performed an exceptional landing.

"You all right?"

Her muscles felt stiff but, other than that, she was all right. She nodded.

"Sure?"

A man with dark skin, and hair black as the night sky, rushed toward them, flashlight casting shadows all around. His face was alive with excitement. He grabbed the pilot's door and threw it open. "Ah! Señor Ace. I saw a plane trying to land like a crazy dodo bird..." For emphasis, the man spread his arms wide and turned a circle on the ground. "... I knew it had to be you." He grinned, sporting a hole where front teeth usually resided.

"Hola, mi amigo," Ace responded easily, shutting down the engine.

"Ah, Señor Ace, you brought company." He punched Ace in the arm. "Is about time. Me and my wife, we think it will never happen. Welcome, lady, welcome."

He reached across Ace, extending a hand. Ace pushed the man's hand back. Nicole frowned at Ace.

"Perhaps I should make some introductions, first. Ricardo, this is Nicole Jackson. With WorldNet. Nicole, my friend, Ricardo Maldanado."

Ricardo quickly dropped his hand to his side, as if the threat of her touch offended him. She turned the full force of her scowl on Ace. He'd known this would happen. But why? She wanted answers. Now.

"Later, Nicole," he promised. "You can have a piece of me later."

"You bring her here?" Ricardo demanded, waving his arms like the dodo bird he'd spoken of. "Are you loco? This is too much, even for you."

"What did you want me to do? Kick her out of my plane?"

"That would be better than bringing her here, no?"

"I don't think the lady likes parachutes."

"No. No." The man frantically shook his head, then glanced over his shoulder, his wide-eyed alarm clear. "Is too dangerous, Señor Ace. You must take her away. Pronto."

A shiver of fear, unlike anything she'd ever felt, started at the base of her spine and spiked its way up, until it shimmered at her nape. "No," Nicole said. She clutched Ace's biceps and felt the tension coiled in solid muscle. She'd come too far; her future, and everything she'd always worked for, was on the line. She couldn't quit. Couldn't lose. "I must meet with Governor Rodriguez. Please."

Because it vanished so quickly, she might only have imagined the momentary melting in Ace's glacier-cold eyes.

"Relax, Ricardo. I'll take care of the *señorita.*"

The man shook his head in jerky motions. "No, no. Is too risky."

"That's my business, Ricardo. Besides, the lady here knows what she's getting herself into."

Under the faded shirt he wore, she felt Ace's muscles bunch and constrict. "Tell that lazy brother of yours to get his butt over here with the taxi."

Ricardo clasped his hands together in the motion of prayer and lifted them heavenward. He rolled his eyes. *"Madre de Dios."*

"You'll be meeting Her soon enough if you don't do as I say, Ricardo. ¿*Comprende*?"

"Ah, *sí, sí.*" He bobbed his head, then hurried away.

With the man's absence, the cockpit felt even smaller, the air lightning-charged. Frogs croaking and crickets chirping provided the only relief from the eerie silence.

"Satisfied?"

Ace had put himself on the line for her. And she had the uncomfortable feeling his help came with a price.

He turned slightly, his muscle flexing. She realized her hand was still wrapped around his upper arm. With a start, she unfurled her fingers and pretended the queasy feeling deep inside was from the flight and Ricardo's strange reaction, and not from the powerful effect Ace exacted on her.

"I didn't lie, did I? You really do know what you're getting yourself into? You know what you're up against?"

"You?" she asked, strangely breathlessly.

"Me?" He shook his head. "Hell, honey, I'm the least of your worries."

His voice contained a grainy undercurrent of urgency that made her uneasy.

"A lot of people don't want you here, Nicole. That should have been obvious by the meeting you just had with my friend. I can guarantee you my enemies won't be so gracious."

"What's going on here?" Tendrils of apprehension held her in their grips.

"A small revolution, Nicole. Sparked by you and your client."

She gulped and the blood drained from her face.

"Ricardo's right. If you had any sense, we'd get the plane refueled and be outta here before anyone knows you ever landed. You can be safe and sound in your bed, probably in your penthouse apartment, before another sun sets.''

Ace shifted. The hilt of his knife reflected prisms of light from the faint runway lamps. She was in a hostile land, entrusting her life to a virtual stranger. Ace hadn't candy-coated facts. Though the governor extended an invitation, others wouldn't be so kind.

And the man she'd hired to help her wasn't on her side. Fear was suddenly very real and very intimidating.

She heard the crank of a car's engine and loud oaths. After several tries, the engine caught, choked, then rushed on. A moment later, a taxi with a missing headlight and twisted fender screeched to a halt beside the plane.

Ace leaned forward, his shoulder brushing the softness of her breast.

His presence disturbed her, made her undoubtedly aware of being a woman. Made her fear she would never again recoup the control she'd lost to her enigmatic protector.

She sucked in a breath. Deeply.

When he sat back up, she saw something glimmer in his hand. Her heart missed a beat.

In his palm, Ace cradled a large pistol. Dread coiled deep inside.

"It's your call, Nicole.''

Three

"**W**ell?" Ace watched while a war of indecision waged on her suddenly pale face. He'd scared her. Intentionally. Cabo de Bello was beautiful. Deceptively beautiful.

The governor had managed to keep the opposition subdued...so far. But for how long was anyone's guess.

He saw Nicole shove away the fear and force grim determination in its place. She'd set a goal and refused to be deterred. It was a noble, if stupid, trait. The same kind of naïveté had gotten him into trouble. Thank God he was too old for that anymore.

"I want to stay."

"Yeah. I expected as much," he said. "Let's go."

After grabbing his small arsenal of weapons, the duffel and her suitcase, he joined her on the tarmac.

Ricardo and his brother, Poncho, glared, and Ace scowled at both men, patience at an end, and snapped,

"Ricardo, put my plane in a hangar. I don't want anyone knowing we're here."

"Por favor, Señor—"

Ace cut off protests with a wave. A lot of islanders didn't want WorldNet's progress. Sweatshop working conditions were good for no one, except owners.

Yet here he was, with a woman who represented each of the things Ricardo and Poncho hated.

Nicole's appointment with Governor Rodriguez wasn't until the morning. Since Ace and Nicole would both have rooms in the mansion, Ace planned to make use of each minute. And as he'd told her, he intended to use whatever tactics he needed. Fair. And foul.

Slyly, he grinned.

Why fly to Rosie's when he had Nicole? After all, he'd felt a response ripple through her when he'd outlined the length of her cheekbone. She'd fought it, but her breath had caught. She was aware of him, just as he was aware of her.

"Ready?" he asked Nicole.

She nodded.

Poncho and Ricardo exchanged uneasy glances, then Ricardo shrugged as if in hopelessness. After tucking his gun into his waistband, Ace turned to see Nicole slide into the taxi gracefully. No easy trick, he knew.

"Watch the hole," he warned. "Part of the floor on that side has rusted through."

"Oh." She glanced at the floor before crossing her long legs.

Poncho climbed behind the wheel and swore several times in Spanish. The car jerked and a groan tore from Nicole's lips.

"Are you all right?"

"Just feeling a little wear and tear," she said.

Ace leaned over the seat and tapped Poncho on the shoulder. "Take it easy, *mi amigo.*"

"*Sí, sí,* I try, I try."

He sat back. "It's only a few miles to the governor's mansion."

She managed a brave smile.

He couldn't summon an answering frown. She had guts and tenacity in equal measures. He'd summed her up quickly when she'd stepped onto the Southern California tarmac. Although she'd been reminiscent of Elana, there'd been several subtle differences.

Sure, Nicole had all the trappings of a spoiled rich girl, from the diamond studs in her ears all the way down to designer aerobic shoes, but there was something more. She carried herself with determination, mixed with an enchanting, exciting vulnerability. Wariness and hurt showed in her face—he'd had plenty of experience recognizing both—even though she fought to hide it. All combined to intrigue him.

An urge to protect her nearly overwhelmed him. And the only thing that stopped him from reaching for her hand was the certainty she wouldn't welcome it.

The car hit a pothole that jarred Ace's teeth. Yet, stoically, Nicole never uttered a word, even when he saw her top teeth sink into her lower lip.

With each mile they drew closer to the governor's mansion, Ace's senses sharpened. He felt as though a hundred pairs of eyes stared at him, tracking every move.

Waiting. Watching.

Unconsciously, he reached for his gun. He cut a glance out the window, seeing swaying trees and low hanging clouds.

"What's the matter?"

Her nervous voice intruded. Never looking at her, he forced a lie. "Nothing."

"Then why are you playing with your gun?"

"I'm not." Even in the shrouding darkness, he knew she'd arched an auburn brow. He frowned, realizing his fingers were resting protectively on the deadly coldness of his weapon. "Nothing's wrong," he reasserted. "Habit."

The disbelief of her gaze penetrated the distance.

"You make a habit of playing with your gun, Mr. Lawson?"

"Ace," he corrected. Again. "The name's Ace. My dad's Mr. Lawson." He'd said it to distract her from her line of questioning, yet, for a second, he actually wondered what his name would sound like when her tongue curled around the word.

"*Ace,*" she said dutifully.

The sensation of a fist landed in his stomach. Lord, she made it sound seductive, just as he'd hoped—just as he'd feared. He groaned. If his name sounded that good, how would it feel to have her tongue on *his,* tasting, testing, teasing?

Shaken, he dragged a hand through the cropped length of his hair. Business, he reminded himself. Nicole was business. And he was a professional.

But his thoughts strayed to the upcoming night ahead. Business. Right. Sure. He'd sworn to do whatever it took to change her mind. Do it he would.

He shifted uncomfortably, his jeans suddenly too tight.

Poncho rounded a corner and slowed down. Ace ruthlessly shoved aside his thoughts as the governor's unkempt lawn and gardens loomed in the taxi's dirty headlight. In the month since Ace's last visit, natural vegetation had choked the life out of the carefully planted gardens. There were no signs of activity.

Ace leaned forward. "What's going on, *mi amigo?*"

The man shrugged several times. *"No sé."*

Ace rubbed the stubble on his chin. He'd spoken to Juan Rodriguez only two weeks ago. The man was anxious to meet Nicole. So where were the lights and welcoming committee?

Poncho stomped on the brake. The car jerked to a stop, spewing pebbles and dirt in every direction.

"Ace?"

Alone, he would have gone inside. But because of Nicole, he refused to take the chance.

Hairs on the back of his neck stirred in undeniable warning. "Turn around, Poncho. Get the hell out of here."

Tires squealed as Poncho forced the manual steering to perform a feat it wasn't designed for.

"What's going on?" Nicole asked in a breathless whisper, evidently confused, obviously reading his panic.

On the back of Poncho's seat, Ace beat an impatient staccato with his fingers. Mentally, he listed possibilities and options. He was aware of the nervous looks Poncho cast in the rearview mirror. "The governor was expecting us," Ace said finally.

"You think something's wrong?"

He nodded tightly. "I do."

She fell silent for a few moments, moments he needed in order to think. A cloud sauntered away from the moon, affording him the opportunity to see her fingers were tightly knotted in her lap. Yet she didn't say anything. Again he found a reason to admire her.

Dragging his attention away from Nicole, he cataloged the things that didn't make sense. Leaning forward, he quietly asked Poncho, "Who knew I was coming here?"

"Señor Rodriguez."

"Anyone else?"

The man met Ace's gaze in the rearview mirror. "Even I did not know, until Ricardo tell me tonight."

The answer only raised more questions. Acid churned in his stomach. The rebels were obviously more of a threat than Rodriguez or Ace had thought.

"I take you to *mi casa,* no?" Poncho offered.

"Gracias, mi amigo." Ace knew they would be somewhat safe with his friends, a whole lot safer than if they strung a hammock between two palm trees.

"Is his home big enough for us?" Nicole asked quietly.

"No." Ace wondered how she would react to an evening of camping out on the home's dirt floor. The first time he'd stayed with the Maldanados, he'd thought of Elana. He knew the idea of spending five minutes in the house would have made her painted toes curl in her satin pumps.

Would Nicole's reaction be any different?

"Is Poncho married?"

"With five kids." He waited for a reaction. Lord knew, his ex had had definite problems when he'd mentioned kids. "Five noisy kids." Ace wished he could see Nicole's expression. Would her lips be curled in disgust at the thought of what having five kids would do to her career, not to mention her figure?

The issue of children had been the first of many to cause serious problems between him and Elana. He

wanted kids—had a desperate burn in his gut to right the wrongs inflicted by his family.

But that wasn't to be. Sometimes he felt a pang of regret, but he'd learned to live with it, by risking his life so children could live longer.

"I hope Mrs. Maldanado won't mind the extra people."

"She probably won't even notice," Ace said wryly.

Poncho jerked the car to a sudden stop in front of a small shack. Ace climbed out and went around to Nicole's side. It was now or never.

"Let me help you," he said, opening her door. She placed her much-smaller hand in his palm. Awareness pulsed through him. It was as shocking as it was unwelcome.

Instead of letting her go as he knew he should, he closed his fingers around her hand, holding her captive.

Her eyes opened wide, bringing her gaze back around until it locked on his face. Neither said a word. Her breathing deepened. His did the same. Her lips—soft, full, sensual—parted in silent invitation.

An invitation he resisted RSVPing to.

What was wrong with him? At thirty-seven, he'd been around the block. So why did the thought of surrendering to the strangeness of night and kissing her bother him?

He'd already said he would do what it took. So why the hesitation? Suddenly the idea of using her gave him qualms. He disliked the flash of conscience.

Poncho cleared his throat, then slammed closed the trunk lid, shattering the illusion of their near intimacy.

"Mi casa," Poncho said apologetically to Nicole.

Ace studied Nicole in the moon's glow. Though the Maldanados' home was rich compared to some on the island, it was poor compared with what she likely called home. To his amazement, she was graciousness itself.

"Thank you for your hospitality, Señor Maldanado." She smiled dazzlingly.

Poncho's face became a wreath of grins. *"De nada, señorita, de nada."*

She had more facets than the two-carat engagement ring Ace had given Elana. And Nicole's smile was more intense. For a second, he allowed himself to imagine what it would feel like to experience its full effect, bestowed on him and no one else.

The shack's door opened with a groan. He wondered if the facade would crack once she saw the five kids, two dogs, three cats and a dozen or so chickens.

But she showed no sign of faltering as a cacophony of sound surged out the door.

"Where's my favorite lady?" Ace demanded, following Nicole inside.

A tall, slender woman, long black hair falling around her shoulders, swung around. "Ace!"

She rushed forward and was swept into Ace's outstretched arms. A strange sensation, something akin to jealousy, snapped at Nicole. Annoyed with herself, she shoved it aside. She had no attachment to Ace and shouldn't care how many women he smashed against his solid chest. Still, when he put down the woman, after only kissing her forehead, Nicole experienced relief.

"Living with this old man still agrees with you, Maria?"

The woman glanced over her shoulder at Poncho, then back at Ace. She winked. *"Sí.* I have not yet found anyone better. Any suggestions, *mi amigo?"*

"Yeah. Me."

Maria laughed, a sweet tinkling sound that Nicole couldn't duplicate if she were paid.

On the fringes, Nicole marveled at the easy camaraderie between Ace and the Maldanados. She had numerous friends and acquaintances, some of them very close, yet she'd never been part of this type of genuine affection. Growing up, she was her father's princess, a pampered child who'd eventually tired of adoration, scared that if she failed, she would no longer be liked.

"Maria, let me introduce Nicole Jackson." The rich timbre of Ace's voice startled her from her reverie.

Maria turned with a smile. "Welcome, Señorita Jackson."

"Thank you." This kind of friendship was new. Despite the friends she had at home, a tug of isolation assailed her.

Ace cleared his throat and cocked his head to one side. "Nicole is CEO of WorldNet."

Maria blinked, her gaze taking in her husband and Ace.

Nicole shifted, unaccustomed to the hostility the name of her company caused.

Maria found her composure and then wiped her hands on her apron. "You'll join us for dinner?"

"And for the night, if possible."

"You and Señorita Jackson are most welcome."

Just then the door burst open and a handful of children swarmed through.

"My children," Maria explained, issuing a command for them to be silent.

"*¡Tío* Ace!"

"Who's that?" demanded a boy of about four, tugging on Maria's apron.

"My name's Nicole," she said, bending to look the child in the eye. "What's yours?"

When the boy stuck out his tongue, Maria scolded him.

"It's okay," Nicole said. The woman's expression softened and distrust faded from her eyes. Nicole looked at Ace. He leaned against a chair, in a casual, yet all-alert gesture. He reminded her of a predator, waiting to pounce on his prey.

Nicole shivered.

She was his prey.

"Hey, sport," Ace said, finally moving. In two easy strides, he crossed the room. He picked up the child and tossed him into the air. "The lady's with me." Ace tickled Pedro's ribs. "You don't have a problem with that, do you?"

The boy squirmed and giggled. "No, *Tío* Ace."

Nicole wondered at Ace's knack with children. They seemed to revere him, even giving him the honorary Spanish title of "uncle." The Ace she'd glimpsed hadn't seemed the type to chuck a child under the chin. Yet he was a natural. She wondered if he had any kids of his own.

After that, the atmosphere became one of a carnival. Children played loudly, animals barked and clucked, and the adults shouted to be heard over the noise. Sitting around a wooden table after dinner, Nicole realized it felt good to be surrounded by the Maldanados and their obvious love for one another. Even when one of the children did something wrong, Maria still showed her affection.

Maria stood to wash the dishes and Nicole joined her, gathering plates.

"Is not necessary," Maria said. "I will be done soon."

"Sooner if I help," Nicole said, unbuttoning the pearls at her wrists and rolling up the silk sleeves.

Nicole felt Ace track her every movement. She resisted the impulse to turn around and meet his eyes.

Nearly an hour later, Maria was busily involved in getting the children ready for bed. Maria grabbed a tattered book and her children gathered around her. Just then, the youngest began to wail. With a deep sigh of reluctance, Maria put down the book and reached for the baby.

"Do you want me to try?" Nicole offered, although she had no idea what she could do to help.

Maria shook her head, though she smiled gracefully. "This one, he likes his mama."

"Then I'll read the story."

"It's in Spanish," Maria said gently.

"That's okay," Nicole persisted. "I'll read it to them."

"You speak Spanish?"

"And several other languages. It helps in my career."

Maria nodded, then smiled. "In that case, my thanks."

Nicole took the seat Maria had occupied, very conscious of Ace standing near the door, a shoulder casually propped against the jamb.

She started into the story, embellishing as she went along. One by one, she enchanted the children, feeling a pang of regret that she'd never experienced the same thing. As much as she'd begged him to, her father had never read her any stories. Though he'd denied none of the toys, then cars and clothes she'd asked for, he'd never given her the one thing she'd craved more than anything as an only child: time.

There'd been no extra hours for stories or for attending a pretend tea party with her teddy bears. When she had kids—if she had kids—she mentally corrected, small things like that would be important.

Finally she closed the book. The kids, judging by loosely hanging jaws and wide eyes, had enjoyed the story as much as she had.

"Impressive," Ace said.

She glanced up, entrapped by the sardonic look on his face. "Surprised?"

"Yeah," he admitted, strong shoulders resting on the wall behind him.

"It was just a story," she said, dismissing both the tension and the fluttering inside. Nicole experienced a thrilling sensation of satisfaction. Her work hadn't afforded her the pleasure that spending time with the Maldanados' children had. Nicole realized she would long remember the feel of a small hand resting on her leg.

Nicole stood, smoothing wrinkles from her clothing and pretending not to notice the way her hands trembled.

Ace pushed away from the wall and vanquished the distance between them with a few easy strides. Stomach knotted, Nicole met him, stare for stare. Purpose and intent glittered in his eyes. Her shoulders stiffened in involuntary reaction to the predatory aura he exuded.

"You can use our room," Maria said, her quiet voice shattering the tension building between Nicole and Ace.

"Nonsense," Nicole protested, dragging her gaze away and sucking in a steadying breath. "I wouldn't dream of having you move out of your room." Much as

she tried to think of the implications of sharing a bedroom with a man of his potency, his barely suppressed
masculinity, her mind irrepressibly painted images.
Thrilling, chilling images.

"But you and Ace will need the privacy."

She gulped and noticed the way Ace just continued to
regard her. His features were indecipherable. He hadn't
moved, made no effort to rescue her. He seemed content to watch her flounder. "No, no, we'll be fine out
here."

"Nicole's right," Ace said, finally facing Maria.
"We've caused you enough inconvenience."

When Maria started to protest, Ace held up his hand,
demanding silence. "Nicole and I will sleep out here."

"Very well," Maria agreed, obviously realizing she
wasn't going to win this battle. "I'll get some blankets."

"I'll give you a hand," Nicole offered, intent on
fleeing Ace's presence.

Maria shook her head. "No need."

Nicole made herself busy, straightening a few toys,
then rearranging the same items. Poncho and Ace were
seated on the worn couch and she felt conspicuous.
She'd spent years in boardrooms, led discussions and
debates, even entertained foreign dignitaries. But no
experience left her prepared for the way her stomach
knotted under the hot intensity of Ace's scrutiny. Did
the man show no mercy?

Finally Maria returned, a few blankets stacked in her
arms. "I'm sorry I haven't an extra bed to offer,
but—"

"This is perfect," Nicole said, standing to take the
armload of linens. "You've been more than kind."

Maria swept away coffee cups, then she and Poncho bid Ace and Nicole good-night and left the room. The door swooshed gently closed. Suddenly she and Ace were alone. The room shrunk. The air cracked with tension. And Nicole wished she were anywhere but here, with this overwhelming man.

She sank onto a chair and set down the blankets. Anger, frustration and helplessness gnawed at Nicole, the events of the previous twenty-four hours taking their toll. In less than a day, she'd flown in a ridiculously small airplane, had her plans to meet Governor Rodriguez thwarted, ended up accepting the hospitality of people she didn't know and been continually stared at by Ace Lawson.

How much more could she endure?

She wrapped her arms around her middle, struggling to keep the consuming emotions from destroying her self-confidence. "Why do you keep waiting for me to fail?"

Ace looked up, steepled his fingers, but didn't respond.

"You disliked me on sight."

He cocked his head, acknowledging her statement.

"And that's not fair. You want me to say the wrong thing, act the wrong way. Well let me tell you, Mr. Hotshot Pilot..." She drew in a ragged breath when he tugged his gun from his waistband.

"Do you really want Maria and Poncho to hear this?" he asked softly, checking the gun's ammunition clip.

She glanced over her shoulder, seeing just how thin the walls really were. "No."

"Good. Then let's go outside. I promised you earlier you could have a piece of me. Seems like you want it now."

His calm reasoning deflated her, as if a gust of wind receded, leaving her unsteady and uncertain.

He stood, and her gaze focused on his Adam's apple. Though they were almost the same height, Ace Lawson was one of the few men who actually made her feel small.

"Come on," he said after securing his gun and grabbing a flashlight from the duffel bag.

"Where are we going?"

"To the beach."

"Is it far?"

"A ten-, maybe fifteen-minute walk."

"Is it safe?"

"That's what I want to find out."

Despite the warm Caribbean breeze, frozen tendons traced her spine. Not for one minute could she forget that this wasn't a pleasure trip.

In reality though, she hadn't expected trouble. She thought she and the governor could work out an agreement and she could fly home, her firm's future secure.

She shivered.

In an instant, Ace was behind her, grabbing his jacket and holding it for her. She accepted it, aware that the soft, faded denim possessively held his scent. Still, though it was large, it conformed to her, wrapping her warmly.

"Thanks," she said.

"Just doing my job, ma'am. Wouldn't want you to get pneumonia. At least not until you're back in the States."

"And not your responsibility anymore?"

"Right."

Once the door closed behind them, Ace flicked on the flashlight's narrow beam. "Outhouse is over there," he said, directing the light to the right. "Need to go before we take our walk?"

"Do you have to be so crass?"

"Look, lady, you don't know the meaning of the word. Giving you a chance to use the facilities before we leave is not crass. Asking if you need to take a leak in the ocean, now *that's* crass."

Nicole rolled her eyes. Ace Lawson embodied the word *crass,* from the way he dressed in faded jeans and worn leather, to the way he smiled in a sexy, seductive manner.

"Well, do you need to go?"

She frowned. "Yes."

"I'll go with you."

"Give me a break, Mr. Lawson. I can go to the ladies' room by myself."

"Ladies' room? That's not a ladies' room, that's an outhouse."

"Semantics."

"Oh, yeah?"

"When was the last time you and your *semantics* saw a snake in a rest room?"

A cold chill crept into her heart. *Snake.* She'd hated snakes since Tommy James put a garden snake in her first grade desk. When she'd opened her desk to get a pencil, she'd grabbed the reptile instead and pulled it out. She still remembered the way the body swayed back and forth in her chubby grip like a live electrical wire. She'd screamed as the wicked, forked tongue darted in and out and the beady eyes glared accusingly at her. After nearly squeezing it in two, she'd dropped it and it had slithered over her black patent shoe, leaving a sticky, slimy trail from the spilled glue on the floor.

"Are you coming or what?"

She looked over to where Ace stood, the privy door ajar. Suddenly she didn't need to go anymore.

"No, I'll, er, use it when we get back."

Across the starlit night, she heard him sigh. "Suit yourself."

Nicole caught up to him after he turned a corner. They walked in silence along the narrow, rutted road. With each step, the scent of the sea became stronger. In the silence, she heard the rush and ebb of the tide, the rustle of wind through trees and bushes, and the alternately rasping chirps and piercing whine of cicadas. It was surprising how bright it was under the half-moon and a canopy of stars, as though it were twilight instead of midnight.

She stepped in a rut and stumbled. The anger that had been receding in the peaceful surroundings began to inch closer. Everything was Ace's fault. His fault she was walking in the middle of the night, instead of sleeping. His fault her meeting with Governor Rodriguez had been postponed.

"You're mad again," Ace said when they reached Cabo de Bello's majestic shore.

Instead of responding, she stood there, captivated. Though she lived in California, she rarely visited the ocean. She'd forgotten how spectacular it could be.

Ace took hold of her arm and guided her toward the gurgling surf.

His touch brought the emotional cauldron back to the surface. "You're very perceptive." She tried not to notice the way his fingers cupped her elbow as if made for that purpose.

"Let's have it."

Nicole pulled her arm back, needing to think. She stood only inches away from him and the lapping waves. "You set me up with Poncho, then again with Maria."

"If you can't handle yourself with my friends, how are you going to handle the others who don't want you to succeed? And how in the hell do you expect to win over the rebels with machine guns?"

"You were testing me?" she asked incredulously, pushing errant strands of auburn hair off her face.

"Yep. You get a B-. You're gonna have to bring it up to an A-. Not everyone is as patient as me."

"Patient? That's the last word I'd use to describe you."

"I imagine you have a few choice words in mind."

His T-shirt billowed in the breeze and she had to fight the urge to tuck it in more securely. "I do," she said through a mouth that had gone dry.

"Any more complaints, Ms. Jackson?"

"Plenty."

"I'm all ears."

"The way you landed."

"Lady, no one could have done any better. No one. That runway was wrecked by a hurricane."

"But Ricardo..."

"It was an inside joke."

"A joke?" she asked.

"That's right. Anything else?"

She nodded.

"Go for it."

"Your attitude toward me."

"Go on." He grinned.

"You don't like me."

"Wrong." He stuffed a hand in a pocket. "I don't like what you're here for. I checked out your company. Some of the deals you've pulled off for your clients in Japan are outstanding. I think WorldNet offers a valuable service—as long as the nation you're dealing with wants the kind of progress you're pedaling. But Cabo de Bello doesn't."

"The governor does."

"The man was elected to office, yes," Ace agreed. "But there's no telling how long he'll last. Believe it or not, most people sympathize with the rebels because they represent the way the majority feels. *They don't want you.*"

Tightly contained fury pulsed from him, hanging in the tropical night. It simultaneously frightened and fascinated her. Attracted as well as repelled her.

"If you feel this strongly, you shouldn't have brought me here."

"I gave it a lot of thought. But I needed the money. It's a screwy part of life. Even if you try to live on principles, you've got to find a way to fund those beliefs. Believe me, darlin', if I didn't think I had a chance to help change your mind, I wouldn't have agreed. I want your defeat, Nicole, your abject, on-your-knees surrender."

"And you'll do anything to ensure it."

"Yes."

She shuddered. His intensity shook her to the core.

"I'll win, Nicole." He said the words softly, with a hint of menace.

Nicole drew on her mental reserves, built over a lifetime of dealing with determined males. She refused to cower. "Like you said, it's not a game. This is real life and you're just my pilot. For crying out loud, you don't even live here. I'm through listening to your personal propaganda."

He reached for her and his fingers sank into the tender flesh of her upper arm. "You're paying me, but only because *I* agreed. There wasn't anything in that contract that gave you authority to dictate my thoughts. I don't work for you or WorldNet. Don't mistake that. I work for myself.

"And I'll do everything I can to stand in your way. That's a promise."

He released her and the sudden loss made Nicole's shoulders sag.

"But it's not for you to say, is it?" she asked, trying desperately to cover the fact he'd successfully cut through her barriers.

"Yeah, darlin', it's for me to say, because I happen to be the only one in a position to reason with you."

"But you're not being reasonable. And you obviously don't understand business. If you did, you'd realize Cabo de Bello's economy is dirt-poor. My client is offering an economic boost these people need . . . fast. Any fool can see that."

"Then I guess I'm a fool, because I don't see it. If your client was offering an economic boost, they'd be offering a forty-hour work week with overtime pay and benefits. They wouldn't be offering laughable wages for a fifty-hour week in substandard working conditions."

"The details of the arrangement are my client's."

"Then they sure as hell should be your business."

"And what would you know of business, Mr. Lawson?"

"There's more to life than money, honey. I pity you for not having the ability to see beyond the color green."

The breeze lifted and tossed his hair. His forehead was lined with intensity, a reflection of his inner conviction.

"I learned about dollars and cents the hard way. I was in business, Nicole. And I didn't like it. I get more rewards now than I ever thought possible."

His forehead relaxed with his words and it was as though the tension dissipated like a patch of fog.

"And you're wrong about another thing, Nicole. I like you. A lot. Maybe too damn much. And maybe that's why it's so important to get you to listen. I think you're inherently good, even though you try and bury it under layers of business bull."

When he reached for her again, she was helpless to resist. Where his touch had been harsh and uncompromising, it was now tender... exciting.

She couldn't think of anything more to say, and when he started to move his hands, she couldn't think at all. Standing near him, inhaling his sexy scent, watching the lines around his eyes disappear, the furrow on his brow fade, all combined to steal her thoughts, and her anger. And left her to luxuriate in something tender and inexplicable.

"What? Nothing else to say? I can't believe it. Nicole Jackson, president of WorldNet, is at a loss for words." He let out a low, spellbinding whistle. "Wait till the home office gets a load of this. It'll probably make the in-house newsletter."

She couldn't help it. He painted such a ridiculous picture that her air rushed out, making her feel relaxed.

"Ah, so you *can* smile."

Instantly she sobered.

"You should do it more often."

He reached toward her, and she trembled when he eased a strand of hair from her cheek. Her thoughts tumbled over one another in a jumbled mess. They were from two completely opposite worlds; they saw this and probably everything else from different perspectives. Yet she couldn't prevent her heart from thumping or her breath from catching in her throat.

"Ace...don't..."

"I like the way you say my name. Soft, husky."

His thumb pad grazed her dry lips.

"Say it again."

She did.

"Has anyone uncovered your woman's passion, Nicole?"

Her heart tripped at the way her name so sensually rolled off his tongue.

"Hmm?" he asked.

"Don't," she pleaded. "Don't do this to me."

"Has anyone taken the time to awaken you? Have they?"

"No," she whispered, the admission painful.

"Maybe it's time someone did."

His voice, so quiet, lazily drifted through the salty air. Then his hand pressed against her nape. A fraction of an inch at a time, he drew her closer until all she inhaled was his masculinity and all she heard was the swirling rhythm of their combined heartbeat.

Damn the man.

The warmth of his tongue replaced the calluses of his thumb. With lazy flicks, his tongue outlined the curved shape of her mouth.

Nicole had never experienced such a sensuous onslaught before. Nothing in her experience prepared her for the feelings his touch aroused.

Ace tugged the pins from her chignon. Her hair tumbled, floating around her shoulders and teasing her neck. Pins clinked together when they landed on the damp, sandy ground.

"Gorgeous," he said against her mouth, threading his fingers through the strands. He inhaled deeply. "Always wear it this way."

He said he intended to change her mind, use whatever tactics it took to win. But when his tongue asked for entrance to her mouth, resistance fled. She recognized that she was in the arms of an enigmatic stranger, a stranger urging her to give in to the seductiveness of the moon-streaked night.

Though she'd never done anything like this before, and despite knowing it was nothing more than persuasion to him, she was lost.

She might regret it later, but for now she wrapped her arms around his neck and melded her body with his. In invitation, she opened her mouth.

He groaned, a heavy, guttural sound that inflamed her, compelling her to give more.

Their tongues joined in an erotic dance. He tasted; she teased. She probed; he plundered.

Her breaths were ragged as he took everything she offered, then demanded more.

She felt a bead of perspiration, more from excitement than exertion, trace down her back and pool into the satin of her panties.

"Sweet Lord," Ace said, slowly ending the kiss.

Her mouth was swollen and heavy with need. He cradled her waist, holding her captive still.

"Don't look at me that way," he commanded.

She licked away his moisture from her bottom lip, drawing it deep inside, savoring the taste of him.

He moaned.

She smiled, heady with the power that he wanted her as badly as she wanted him. "What way?"

"Like you'd welcome me into your bed."

Nicole shivered. Fact was, right now, she *would* welcome him into her bed. And that scared her. She never acted without considering all possible repercussions.

"We'd better get back."

Unable to find the words to voice her agreement, she nodded. He took hold of her elbow possessively. And she didn't mind.

It wasn't until they'd left the sparkling sand behind that she realized Ace had awakened her woman's passion more surely than any man she'd ever known.

Suddenly she was afraid, scared of losing control, scared of losing the account, scared of Ace using his powers of persuasion to change her mind, scared nothing would ever be the same again....

Four

"Go ahead and take the couch," he said.

"That's all right. You can have it."

She'd whispered, apparently so as not to disturb their hosts. She was the most obstinate, infuriating woman he'd ever met. He refused to acknowledge the nagging voice that told him he was more annoyed with himself and his physical discomfort than with Nicole. "You're shorter than me."

"Only by about three or four inches."

"Do you have to argue about everything?"

"I never argue, I—"

"Proved my point."

A soft sigh escaped between her lips as she wiped back a lock of hair that had fallen across her eyebrows. He resisted the compulsion to wrap it around his finger.

"Okay, Ace, you win. I'll sleep on the couch."

She grabbed a blanket and crossed to the lumpy sofa.

He wondered if she intended to sleep in her clothes or just a T-shirt. Though the idea of seeing the long length of her legs held a certain appeal, he didn't think he would be able to deal with the physical ramifications. Their kiss had already slammed his hormones into overdrive.

She climbed beneath a blanket. Fully dressed. Ace lay awake for a long time, listening to the gentle sounds as she shifted and plumped a pillow. It had been a long time since he'd had a woman curled in his arms, even longer since the woman had meant anything special. He wondered what it would feel like to have Nicole's hair spill across his neck, his shoulders, his chest.

And he wondered what would have happened if she wasn't fighting for something he vehemently opposed. Irritated, he rolled over and swore savagely as a splinter sank into his hip.

"Ace?"

Lord, how was it possible for a woman's voice to sound so husky?

"Are you asleep?"

Not a single part of his anatomy was asleep. "Yeah."

"I thought I heard something outside."

She sat up and he saw the moon's glow illuminating each strand of her hair, as if kissed by a star.

"There it is again." She clutched the blanket to her breast. "Didn't you hear it?"

He hadn't. And he'd been listening. But, to assuage the fear in her voice, he turned back over, pulling out the splinter before pushing to his feet.

A warm breeze drifted off the Caribbean, swirling around his chest as he crossed to the mosquito-net-covered window. He saw nothing. A cloud ambled away from the moon and, when he faced her, he read her apprehension. "No boogeymen," he promised, allowing the netting to drift back into place. "Feel better?"

"A little. Thanks."

She lay back down and he did the same. A few minutes later, an unearthly screech split the night silence. Nicole whimpered and curled into a self-protective ball.

Again, the long-dormant urge to protect walloped him. He was unprepared for its intensity. She wasn't his type. Painfully, his ex-wife had taught him the lessons of having an independent wife. So why the primal need where Nicole was concerned?

The bird's unholy sound again scraped across the silence. "Nicole," he said softly, "come here. It's all right to need someone sometimes."

She remained rigid. Determinedly, he stood, crossed to the couch and scooped her into his arms; her legs curled over his arm and her derriere pressed against his waist.

"What are you doing?" she asked.

"Sleeping with you."

She gasped.

"Sleep, sweetheart, sleep. Nothing else," he promised, though he wanted to do a whole lot more than hold her.

He laid her on the floor and dropped down beside her. She didn't protest when he pulled her bottom against his body.

A bed would have been nice, he thought. But since he'd met Nicole Jackson, nothing had gone as he planned. He hadn't expected her to be such a looker, and it would have been a lot easier if she wasn't. A whole lot easier.

A ragged breath made its way from his lungs. It'd been a hell of a day. Adding insult, Nicole wiggled, forcing him to fight for control over his surging testosterone level.

"Ace?"

"Hmm?"

"Thanks."

He nearly said, "You're welcome," but stopped short; he wasn't a hypocrite. She was thanking him for his protection. And right now she needed protection from him.

What would she think if she knew?

The part of Ace pressing so hard against her caused Nicole more apprehension than it did comfort. Though her experience with men was limited, she knew Ace Lawson desired her.

As much as she desired him.

And that threatened her hard-won control. She gulped and shifted at the startling thought. Ace muttered and she felt him grow even harder.

"Keep still."

She understood the warning. If she didn't keep still, she wouldn't be safe in his arms.

Nicole froze.

Making love with him would be a mistake of magnificent proportions. They were opposites, from two very different worlds. He opposed what she had to accomplish, and he was blunt in his opinions. And he was as arrogant as Rambo. She told herself that arrogant men didn't appeal to her.

So why did her pulse quicken every time he glanced at her through smoky eyes?

Once she snuggled beneath his chin and used the corded strength of his biceps as a pillow, she no longer heard strange sounds. His heart thumped reassuringly under her ear, and her last conscious thoughts were of security and comfort.

Hours later, muted sounds, of birds chirping, of people whispering, ribboned into her mind. Scents of bacon and coffee wafted in the air; heat and humidity surrounded her like a heavy woolen cloak. But the shadows and fears of the night were gone, vanquished by daylight.

And Ace's arms.

She pried her eyelids apart... and saw the object of her thoughts standing not twelve inches from her, towel draped around his naked shoulders. The ends hung down his chest, a vivid contrast to his skin and mat of dark hair. He wore nothing except a pair of shorts and the towel.

A sudden urge to replace the towel with her hands assailed her. Her fingers would tease his crisp chest hair, then trail lower until they disappeared beneath the indentation of his navel.

She also noted he'd shaved, revealing an oh-so-sexy cleft in his chin. To recover her equilibrium, Nicole closed her eyes again and pretended to be asleep.

"Coffee's on."

She didn't move and hoped her chest rose and fell with the appropriate motions of sleep, rather than in time with her raggedly pounding heart.

The air around her stirred and she caught a whiff of his tropical, spicy scent. Moments later, he whipped the blanket away.

Instinctively, she reached to grab for it, forgetting she was supposed to be asleep.

His chuckle was low and deep. "Anyone ever tell you you're a lousy actress?"

Despite herself, she smiled. It was impossible not to.

"So tell me," he said softly, crouching beside her.

Only inches from her eyes, his thighs strained against the fabric and the front stretched taut across his...

"See anything that interests you?"

"Ace!"

Innocently, he jerked a thumb toward the table. "Maria made breakfast for you."

"Breakfast?"

"Yeah, breakfast. What did you think I was talking about?"

She flushed, from her neck to the roots of her hair.

He grinned lecherously before standing. "Like I said, you're a lousy actress, Nicky."

Nicky. No one, except her father, had ever called her Nicky. And he'd given her the nickname to compensate for the fact that she wasn't a boy. The way Ace said Nicky left no doubt he knew she was a woman. A desired woman.

He offered a hand. A nervous flutter skittered up her spine as he drew her up and continued pulling until her breasts pressed against his bare chest.

Her nipples hardened into tight knots and her breath squeezed from her throat.

She thought last night's magic would have vanished like a sea mist. It hadn't.

Just then the front door banged open and a horde of children swarmed through. Maria followed them in, a bright smile lighting her features.

Nicole pushed away from Ace and felt his muscles contract. She busied herself, smoothing her blouse as she tried to regain her composure. It would be easy to forget she was here on business. Ace's arms were far too comforting; she knew it wouldn't be difficult to surrender to his skilled caresses. No matter what, she had to keep her objectivity, had to remember she was a business person with a mission first, a woman with wants and needs second.

From the kitchen, Ace offered, "Coffee?"

"That'd be nice. Thanks."

Nicole took a few minutes to gather her wits, twisting her hair back into its customary chignon. Shirt tucked in, tennis shoes on and knotted perfectly, not a strand of hair out of place, a fresh coat of foundation and mascara, she felt much better, back in control. When she joined Maria and Ace at the table, it was as if the night and its shared intimacy never existed.

Until Ace's fingers collided with hers.

With a jolt, she looked at him.

She saw it in his eyes. The intimacy had been as real for him as it had for her. Difference was, it shook her, yet didn't seem to bother him, except to prove he intended to win. Even if he hurt and betrayed her in the process.

"You go to the mansion today, no?" Poncho asked.

The smoky color that shrouded Ace's eyes faded, laziness replaced by tension. The sensitive Ace of last night—her Ace—disappeared as if he'd never been.

"Right after breakfast."

The Maldanado children finished their meal, then headed for the door. Little Pedro, so remote and hostile the night before, wrapped his chubby arms around her neck and squeezed hard before running outside to join his brothers and sisters.

A warm tingle filled her at the boy's touch, and she again questioned the way she'd chosen to live her life. She had a career. But at what cost? She'd probably never experience the feeling of holding a baby next to her breast.

Nicole glanced at Ace, and noticed his expression had relaxed. Obviously he would be a great dad. An unfamiliar pang reached her as she again wondered if he already had kids of his own . . . and if they had the same gray eyes that lent a dangerous combination of sex and sin to his expression.

"Well, *mi amigo*," Ace said to Poncho, "You ready to get off your lazy behind or are you taking *siesta* early?"

Poncho slid his mug on the table, then kissed his wife with a passion that surprised, and embarrassed, Nicole. To experience that kind of unhesitating passion . . .

Poncho grabbed the keys and headed outside. Ace zipped his duffel bag and slung it over his shoulder before cutting Nicole a purposeful glance. "Behave yourself."

Without another word he turned to leave. Anger, as swift and fierce as a tropical storm, surged through her, banishing tender thoughts.

In two strides, she caught up to him, wrapping her fingers around his biceps. The look he gave her when he glanced from her hand to her face could have curdled milk.

It did turn the coffee she'd drunk into a gurgling threat. Still, she refused to be left behind.

He raised a brow purposefully and Nicole heard Maria mutter an excuse, then go into her bedroom. Nicole drew from her boardroom experience and refused to be cowed by the fact her fingertips dug into solid male muscle.

Crackling silence charged between them.

"You're staying."

She tipped her head back, feeling the pins securing her hair dig deeper into her scalp. For an uncomfortable second, she remembered the exhilarating thrill she experienced last night when Ace had tugged out the pins, one by óne, and dropped them to the silky sand.

"You can't expect me to wait while you play G.I. Joe."

"Why not? You dress like Barbie. Surely your nails need polishing."

"That's not fair and you know it. I have a job here and I'll be damned if I'll let you stop me from doing it. Need I remind you, you've been well paid to protect me?"

The breath he pulled in, then forced out between his locked lips spoke volumes.

"What the hell. The cemetery's near the governor's mansion, anyway. Let's go."

He clamped his palm around her wrist and applied enough pressure that she released her hold. The imprint of her nails marred his flesh.

The coffee churned again, burning against the back of her throat. She knew it was as much from the warning as from the sizzle when she and Ace clashed. It scared her, and if she was honest, excited her.

She followed him out to the sputtering taxi and slid in beside him, noticing the dirt and grime caked in the cracked vinyl seat. In the daylight, she clearly saw where the floorboard had rusted through. There was a hole beneath her right foot, revealing a large lizard hiding under the car.

Poncho romped on the accelerator, throwing her against Ace. She muttered an excuse, trying not to remember the way it had felt to be wrapped in his arms with the moonlight hanging overhead, or the way he'd cradled her so naturally between his legs.

Nicole's teeth were clenched by the time Poncho turned onto the oiled road that provided the residents of Cabo de Bello with one of their main thorough-fares. With every bone-jarring dip and bump, she forced herself to remember that the well-being of her employ-ees rested on her shoulders.

Palm trees—countless varieties, fronds forming a tropical canopy—lined the road. Plants, rare in other parts of the world, grew wild, their colorful array splashed across the countryside like a priceless patch-work quilt. From her hours of research, she knew the sun kept the bay warm enough for swimming year-round, and yet the heat was rarely oppressive.

Paradise. At least she'd thought so.

Poncho careened around another corner, tossing Nicole against Ace. Their heat met and melded. "Sorry," she murmured.

Except for the momentary highlight in Ace's eye color, she might have imagined the touch didn't bother him. She scooted as close to the rust-rotted door as safety allowed.

As they again turned toward the coast, the salt-scented breeze reached her. And so did the fact that Ace's shoulders became rigid. Already she could read his unease in the way he held his body, in the way a pulse throbbed in his temple.

Ace and Poncho exchanged rapid-fire conversation in Spanish. Though she feigned calm, she couldn't help the panic that rose in her chest at their words.

"What looks out of place?" she asked when they paused.

"No people."

His lack of emotion made icy tendrils creep up her back. She gulped, noticing that manicured gardens had been sacrificed to natural vegetation in an unnatural orgy. A guard, wearing khaki and a mustache stood on the porch, a machine gun hanging from one shoulder. A strange taste stung the back of her throat. Her own fear?

"Get your head down," Ace warned.

Not questioning the tone, for once happy to relinquish control, Nicole did as Ace instructed.

A puff of dust edged through the missing floorboard when Poncho jerked to a halt. Nicole coughed, then cringed as she saw a snake slither, then coil, beneath her.... "Oh, God."

"Please, Nicole, be quiet. For once."

Ace clicked the ammo clip into place, making her heart do double time. He tucked the weapon at the small of his back, inside his blue jeans waistband.

Poncho forced the door open. Seconds passed with agonizing slowness as fatigue wound through her tightened muscles. She felt the pressure of Ace's hand at her nape, but oddly, his rough touch reassured her.

She heard a slam, then with a speed that made her dizzy, her head crashed against Ace's calf. Poncho spun the car around. Dirt gulped through the hole and made her choke and gasp, but Ace kept his fingers tight.

"Ace?" Her panic increased in proportion to the amount of time he continued to squeeze, as though unaware he held her. Finally, consumed with fear, she struggled away. "Talk to me, damn it!"

He stared at her for a long second.

"*¡Madre de Dios!*" Poncho threw up his hands and the car careened to the right.

"Will someone tell me what's going on?" Nicole fought against the rising hysteria. The armed guard, Poncho's reaction and Ace's tight-lipped stare made her queasy.

The men exchanged masculine glances in the rear-view mirror.

Finally Ace broke contact and looked at her. The fact that his eyes were expressionless and lips compressed did nothing to stop the churning nausea. She took a deep breath, forcing cleaner air into her lungs. She knew when he spoke he'd tell the truth. A shiver cascaded through her.

"There's been a change of plan."

"Yes?" Was that her voice, so weak and filled with a tremble?

"Governor Rodriguez is dead."

Five

Nicole felt as though someone grabbed her world and yanked, sending her hopelessly careening. Her heart thundered. "Dead?" she repeated, her voice hardly audible above the car engine's roar. She sank against the rapidly warming seat in disbelief. "Why?"

"I told you there was a faction not interested in progress." Sarcasm lanced his words. "Don't get me wrong. I don't sanction what the rebels did. I liked Rodriguez. Respected him. Believe me, even to stop you and your client, I wouldn't have it happen this way."

Utter defeat clawed at her stomach. She'd made it all the way to Cabo de Bello, only to fail. WorldNet would be squeezed in Sam Weeder's greedy grip.

It was over.

Tears stung her eyes and a lump closed off her throat. She'd failed the hundred people whose careers depended on her success. "I need to send a fax about the situation."

Ace's jaw dropped. "Weren't you listening?"

"I heard," she said. Every single, damning word.

"Do you understand *coup?* This isn't a corporate boardroom, Ms. Jackson, this is a *coup d'état,* with bad guys and guns." He stared at her, long and hard. "A man's dead. You won't be sending any faxes. Anarchy has this funny way of screwing up the phone system."

"I suppose this means we'll be heading back to the States soon." She couldn't help the disappointment gnawing her insides.

Ace grabbed her shoulders, fingertips cruelly biting her skin. "This isn't just about your company, lady. If you remember, we arrived yesterday, with enough fuel remaining to get us off the ground and halfway to the next land mass."

"What are you saying?"

"We're stuck, lady, well and truly stuck."

"Stuck?" The word caught in her throat.

"Stuck. Stranded. Screwed. Call it what you want, the end result's the same. We're not going anywhere until we can take off without anyone knowing you're here."

She went limp in his grip and fought for air. This couldn't be happening. "What are we going to do?"

"I don't know, but pray I come up with something fast."

She did.

Ace released her, and the flesh he'd held tingled.

They sped past scenery that now seemed hostile and threatening...no longer an island paradise.

Ace uttered a sharp command to Poncho. Relief pulsed through her when, a few minutes later, they stopped in front of the Maldanados' home. Amazing how a home that looked so flimsy the night before could now appear to be a fortress.

"Wait here," Ace commanded when she reached for the door handle.

"What? We're not staying?"

He sucked air deep into his diaphragm. "Do us both a favor. Don't argue."

The expression on his face told her not to push him. He was angry, and the way his eyelids narrowed promised he'd throttle her if she didn't listen.

Rays of hot Caribbean sun streamed through the window. Her shirt stuck to her back and her jeans felt as though they'd been humidity-shrunk to fit every curve. As hot as it sometimes was in Los Angeles, the heat didn't feel this oppressive.

Despite his threat, she was about to get out of the car for fresh air when he returned. A backpack hung from his shoulders, and he carried duffel bags and two canteens.

Maria followed him from the hut. "Ace, please."

He opened the back door and tossed in the backpack. "This one has your stuff," he said, handing her one of the bags, then climbing in beside her. Through the pitted windshield, Nicole saw Maria's frantic motions. Even when Nicole laid off employees, she didn't feel as low as she did under Maria's obvious distress.

"Take care," Maria said to Nicole.

"I will." Maria's concern touched Nicole. Though they disagreed philosophically, Maria was generous and kind.

Maria closed the door, then kissed her husband. The Maldanados' unhesitating love served as a painful reminder, again, of what Nicole didn't have . . . and was suddenly afraid she would never have.

Poncho got in the taxi and noisily engaged the engine. They drove for miles, away from the island's capital. Each twist of the road took them to a higher elevation, into the more mountainous region.

Nicole's stomach contorted. She didn't know Ace's plans, but knew she wouldn't like them. She hazarded a glance at him.

His profile was stern. Hard.

Eventually, Poncho pulled off the road, where the vegetation was thick, and towering trees obliterated the horizon.

"We walk from here," Ace said.

"Walk?" she echoed, glancing at her nearly new athletic shoes. She'd already received one blister since leaving California, and the idea of walking any distance was enough to make her toes curl.

"Walk, Nicole. As in one foot in front of the other."

Ace grabbed their belongings, examined his gun, then opened the car door.

Poncho leaned out the side window. *"Vaya con Dios, mi amigo,"* he said, then hastily made the sign of the cross.

Having no way to open the door on her side of the car, thanks to the shrubs rubbing the car's frame, Nicole scooted to Ace's side. The vinyl bore the imprint of his masculine body, and his subtle scent clung to the air.

Ace offered his hand.

The moment their flesh mated, she'd wished she'd used her own power. The flash of recognition that rocketed through her left her shaken. But it was the strange sense of yearning that left her confused.

He'd felt it—whatever *it* was—too. He recoiled as if bitten, dropping her hand.

Ace exchanged a few more words with Poncho, before agreeing, "In one week, then."

The car sped away, the flurry of flying dirt gagging her. She longed for a glass of mineral water on the rocks, with a slice of lime twisted in. A look at Ace's unyielding expression convinced her not to voice her thoughts.

Wistfully she watched the taxi disappear. The car engine's whine faded among the sounds of insects and birds. She was reminded of the time—was it only yesterday?—that her taxi left her at the landing strip.

"Well, lady, here's hoping you like the great outdoors."

"I don't." Except for the one weekend a year she went to Mazatlán, she didn't have time for outdoor fun. She only went to the beach because Doc Morton said she should. Even a weekend each year was too much. She hated the way sand burrowed under her toenails and inside her bikini bottom. Making matters worse, she returned to work sunburned and miserable.

"One week," Ace had said. Did that mean they would be stranded, outside, in the sun and God knew what other elements, with no modern conveniences? A shudder raced between her shoulder blades.

No bathroom. No running water. Just the two of them.

He took her elbow and drew her away from the road. When trees shaded them from the view of passing vehicles, he rolled up her sleeves.

"What are you doing?"

"Protecting you. As you take pleasure in reminding me, that's what I'm being paid for."

He rubbed a sickly smelling insect repellent on her exposed skin before dousing himself.

Ace tugged his knife from its holder and started off through the vegetation. A heavy sigh worked its way from his gut. Not again. He knew there were risks when he scrawled his name across the contract, which was why he'd padded the bill by several thousand dollars.

Should have made it ten. Miss Priss was making him earn every dime, and putting his other operations behind. Damn her and her fool idea of opening a clothing mill.

Sounds of breaking branches and an occasional pseudocurse told him Nicole was right behind. He didn't need to rely on his acute hearing, though.

Despite the danger, he physically responded to her. Her femininity had wound its way inside his body, reminding him just how long it had been . . .

Too damn long. Odd, though, when he thought of making love, it was with Nicole, and he didn't fancy the idea of flying off when dawn inked across the sky.

It grew hotter and damper as the morning dragged on, but he continued his ceaseless pace. Before stopping, he wanted to be sure things were safe.

The sounds of thrashing diminished. Damn it. Ace stopped and checked his watch, trying to determine how far they'd traveled and giving Nicole chance to catch up. He hadn't walked as fast as he would have liked, but she had shorter legs and less stamina. After five minutes of waiting, impatience got the better of him. Shaking his head, he turned and retraced the path he'd taken.

He found her sitting on the vegetation-crippled ground, back resting against a tall tree, knees tucked to her chest. Her bun had fallen loose and long strands of hair hung limply across her cheeks. Her shoes were manure brown and her jeans were mottled with dirt and green chlorophyll.

She glanced up and he recognized her expression: bone-weary exhaustion. In spite of the driving need for safety, Ace couldn't voice the gauntlet-throwing words that would make her spine stiffen and force her to continue.

Huddled like an infant, she looked vulnerable instead of sophisticated. She tugged at something remote inside him, something he believed long since buried.

"I'm sorry... I..." She tried to stand.

After taking a quick survey for reptiles, Ace gently shoved her back to a sitting position. "Rest. You've earned a break."

Sweat weaved down her cheeks, making a disaster of her carefully applied makeup. And damn if she still didn't look appealing.

Ace resisted the urge to hold her and offer false promises of everything working out. She would be grateful, and when he kissed her, would return the passion tenfold. Her slick body would jerk when he touched her... there...

Jeez. He wondered if the weather had affected him, too. He must be really hard up to think of bedding a snooty businesswoman who was more interested in spreadsheets than in spreading the sheets with him.

Ace uncapped the canteen and held it to her mouth. "Not too much," he cautioned.

She took a deep swallow, then offered a wan smile. "Water never tasted so good."

A single drop of water stayed on her lip and Ace wiped it away with his thumb before he had the opportunity to question his motivation. Then, annoyed with himself, he gulped a mouthful.

The metal was warm from her touch.

He twisted the cap on the canteen forcefully. "Ready?"

"How much farther?"

Lord, she really looked tired. He mentally ran through his options. He'd been seen, but she hadn't. The rebels probably wanted to know what he was doing on the island, but as long as they didn't know she was with him...

If he was alone, he would enjoy this hide-and-seek game. But he had to protect Nicole's neck. Ace checked his watch once again. It wouldn't do much good to push her during the heat of the day. Besides, they would make better time when the sun didn't blaze a swath across the cloudless sky.

"You hungry?" he asked.

"No."

"You need to eat, anyway."

He handed her a strip of beef jerky. She took a reluctant bite, then wrinkled her nose.

"It tastes like leather."

"It'll keep you alive." He chewed his own piece of dried beef. She was right; it did taste like leather. He'd forgotten how much he hated the things.

Energy percolated. He hated inactivity, especially when he had forty other things he would rather be doing, such as making a much-needed delivery, arranging for supplies for the next shipment. Instead of doing his part to save the world, he was stuck playing nursemaid to a self-absorbed career woman who looked as if she'd been through the rigors of hell.

And it was barely noon.

It promised to be a real long week.

While she rested, Ace checked the area for vermin, both two-legged and the creepy-crawly variety. Except for insects, and the occasional lizards, all appeared normal.

He dropped the backpack on the ground and took out the bug repellent again. Ace doused himself, then crossed to Nicole. Crouching in front of her, he said, "Time to roll 'em up again."

"Just give me the bottle. I'll do it myself."

"It's easier for me to do it. I can make sure you're completely covered."

Without further protest, she nodded. That made twice in the same day. Good start. Ace took her hand and turned it over. Apparently, he should have reapplied the stuff earlier on Nicole. An insect had already feasted on her wrist.

He squirted a dollop of repellent into his palm. After dipping his fingers in the ointment, he massaged it deeply into her skin. Her flesh was smooth, untanned.

Sexy.

"Thanks."

A flash of something passed between them as he used the balls of his feet to push his body upright.

"Does this mean we're leaving again?"

"If you're up to it." He needed the physical exercise. The jungle-intense heat was short-circuiting his hormonal system. Had to be.

During the next few hours, Nicole stayed close. As the sun slowly slipped across the sky, the intense heat slackened. It hadn't rained but the stickiness made it feel as though it had.

Daydreams about a cold beer, a clean bed and a willing woman tormented him. But it wasn't just any woman he pictured. It was Nicole.... Nicky with her auburn hair loose of its confining knot. It would stream across the pillow, down his naked chest. The silky texture would tease, the scent of her would tantalize.

Her startled yelp dragged him from his pleasantly erotic thoughts. He turned to see her clutching her ankle, a blended mix of pain and accusation on her face.

"You okay?" he asked inanely, hurrying back to her. Of course she wasn't all right. She wouldn't look as though she were ready to fire a bullet into his rear if she was fine.

"No," she said. "I think I sprained it."

He placed one arm around her back, the other behind her knees and swung her into his arms. He tried to shove aside how right it felt to hold her like this. With long strides, he carried her across to a small clearing, then set her on her one good leg—and what a leg, he decided—while he chased some rather large insects off a rock.

After situating Nicole, he knelt. Carefully he worked the laces and pulled apart the shoe leather to expose her foot. She bit her lip as he eased off the high top.

Ace winced in mute sympathy. "Just another second." He tucked his thumb and tugged it off. "Good God." He sucked in a breath. "Why didn't you say something earlier?" Angry red blisters welted her feet.

Obvious pain made her squeeze her eyelids together.

Recrimination washed over him. He was being paid a hell of a lot to take care of her, and so far he was doing a lousy job. He should have stopped for the day and hoped for the best hours ago. And yet, the years of living on the edge had taught him the value of being prepared.

Gently he probed her thickened flesh, feeling for anything broken. Of course, without an X ray it was impossible to say exactly what happened, but it appeared to be a sprain rather than a fracture.

He grabbed the first-aid kit from the backpack. With deft motions that made her clench her hands, he wrapped a bandage around her foot, immobilizing it. Then he opened the antibiotic ointment. She flinched when he rubbed the thick ooze onto her blisters.

She never uttered a word, though.

"Is your other foot as bad?"

Her bottom lip still between her teeth, Nicole nodded. Ace repeated the procedure, then shook his head. Why had she been fool enough to suffer in silence?

Ace taped a few pieces of gauze to her feet, then inched her socks back on. He read the agony in her features. After he finished, she struggled to stand.

"Thanks. I'm ready to go."

He stared at her. She was serious. Despite the twisted ankle and blisters on her feet, she'd offered to keep going. He could hardly believe it. Nicole was proving him wrong, *and proving she wasn't a thing like his ex-wife.*

"We're staying here," he said, tone brusquer than he intended.

"For how long?"

"The rest of the day." Ace unrolled the small nylon tent attached to the backpack. "And the night."

As he prepared the area for the tent, digging trenches and clearing shrubs, Nicole remained strangely silent. Her facial features were pale, probably the result of the sweat washing away what had remained of her painstakingly applied cosmetics.

"Lunch?" He dug packets of ready-to-eat meals from the duffel bag.

"Ick."

"You need to maintain your strength."

With obvious reluctance, she took a package from him.

"How is it?" he asked when she took a bite.

"Edible," she said. "But barely."

He frowned when she refused to eat more than a few bites. She was the most difficult person he'd ever had the misfortune of signing a contract with. Hopefully, island tensions would settle, she would give up her notions of doing business in Cabo de Bello, and he could pilot her back to the security of Southern California. And then he'd wash his hands of her, knowing he'd done his duty.

But as she quietly gritted her teeth and attempted to help with the cleanup, respect built in him. She'd hardly voiced a complaint all day, and she'd followed every order unhesitatingly.

"Rest, because we've got a long day ahead of us tomorrow. I want to put as many miles between us and the rebels as possible."

With obvious reluctance, she nodded and complied. Several times he attempted small talk, only to receive monosyllabic answers.

Through the hundred-year-old trees, Ace watched the rest of the day pass, then slowly yield to night in an artistic array of colors. Why the lack of Nicole talking, combined with the sunset didn't please him, he didn't know. It should have. Generally, he thought she talked too much. This evening, inexplicably, he wanted to hear the sound of her voice.

A covering of clouds played peek-a-boo with the few stars. A half moon hung suspended in the sky to illuminate the night. Except for the plaintive, almost human wail of birds, the air hung still.

Because of Nicole's closeness and the oppressive humidity, sleep would be anything but easy. The tiny three-man tent truly wasn't big enough for two. And he had to share it with his passenger, because he refused to sleep on the jungle ground. Nicole wasn't the only one who hated snakes.

The idea of her bottom curving into him the way it had last night, made him instantly, painfully aware. He'd awoken more than once the previous night, the floral fragrance of her shampoo heightening his senses. Rosie didn't smell like Nicole. And Rosie's ample curves didn't conform to a man the way Nicole's naturally did.

"Do you have a flashlight?"

Her voice carried across the night dragging his mind away from the sexy thoughts.

"Why?"

"I have something to take care of."

"What?"

Silence, steel silence, greeted his question.

"I need something personal from the duffel bag, too."

"Oh." Lord. Ace felt like an idiot for not putting two and two together earlier. Her paleness, fatigue, lack of appetite. He'd figured it was a result of the climate and physical exertion.

But obviously there'd been something more.

Ace thought he'd seen too much of life, too much pain, suffering and human agony to ever be embarrassed. He was wrong. Problem was, he didn't know why.

Maybe because she's a hot woman, Lawson. A hot woman who has stirred passions you thought dead. A hot woman you don't want to keep your hands off. A hot woman who, God knows why, means more than a quick release.

He shoved the unwelcome intrusion away as he turned on the flashlight and went into the tent. For the past few years, he hadn't dealt with a single woman on an emotional level. He hadn't been willing to let anyone close since Elana. His ex-wife's casual statement that their marriage was over if he abandoned the rat race for more rewarding experiences had hurt. Bad. Bad enough not to trust.

He got good sex from Rosie and a couple others in various ports north and south of the Canal. Always he took precautions, left money on the dresser and disappeared before daylight, before physical need translated into emotional attachment.

He emerged from the tent to see Nicole sitting with her legs drawn to her chest. Vulnerable. Needy. Desperate in her own way for love as he.

Somehow, he knew if he didn't get a grip, Nicole would shake his life up as never before.

Six

Mortification threatened to drown her.

In her past relationships, natural female things hadn't bothered her. But with Ace they did. It was humiliating to have to have a man—an incredibly sexy, yet still nearly a stranger—knowing she needed her personal products.

The only saving grace was that after a week she would never see him again; then she could wipe the embarrassment completely from her mind. She shoved aside the feeling of regret that assailed her at the thought of never seeing Ace again. The man was a necessary evil, nothing more. She mentally repeated it again, hoping to convince herself.

"Here."

He handed her the box, rather than the duffel bag as she expected, then offered a flashlight. "Thanks," she mumbled.

"Need anything else?"

She saw him thrust one hand into his jeans pocket. Nicole wondered if Ace was uncomfortable, too. Could he be truly human? "I've got everything I need." Softly she added, "Thank you."

"Yeah, no problem. I'll, er, wait here. There's a place behind that rock that should be pretty private. Yell if anything happens."

A few minutes later, she limped out from behind the rock. He hadn't intruded, stayed a safe distance away, but obviously still close enough.

"Everything okay?"

"Great."

He looked at her, shining the beam from his flashlight directly into her face. "Liar."

"I'm fine, really."

He crossed to her and, seconds later, swept her off her feet. The heat of his arms beneath her knees penetrated denim instantly. Her breath whooshed out and she knew it was from the onslaught of emotions she couldn't name.

She was snuggled against his chest, riding each rise and fall of his breath. A stray lock of hair dropped across his forehead, and she struggled to suppress the urge to finger-comb it back. Nicole didn't question the feeling of rightness that came with being in his arms. Instead, she succumbed, enjoying while she could and knowing it wouldn't last. All too soon he stopped and placed her on a rock. He held her as she slipped down his body. She felt the evidence that he responded to holding her.

"Let me check that ankle."

His ministrations as he pulled off her shoe and then her sock were perfunctory. He directed her to hold the flashlight and didn't glance at her.

"The swelling's going down."

He probed her ankle, then her foot. She squirmed. He did it again. Purposefully, she was convinced.

The night air thickened and insects poured out a mixture of warbled sounds. As Ace rubbed more salve on her blisters, Nicole shivered.

"Cold?"

She wasn't. But the thought of being alone with Ace in the middle of a godforsaken island taken over by rebels made her uneasy. And the overwhelming urge to touch Ace only made matters worse.

Ace finished and the night breeze ruffled his hair, making him look younger, more carefree. She wasn't sure how old he was, but guessed the years hadn't been kind. He acted and had the physical demeanor of a man younger than the crow's-feet etched beside his eyes indicated.

Ace stood, then raked his hair off his forehead. Light had given way to darkness, heat had given way to blessed coolness. Nicole wondered why she still felt so hot.

"Are you hungry?"

Though she had eaten lunch and generally lost her appetite during that time of the month, Nicole discovered that hunger pangs raced through her stomach. "Yes."

"How do you like wild rabbit?"

She frowned. "I don't know. I've never had it."

"Doesn't matter. I probably couldn't catch one anyway."

He smiled, transforming his features, making him appear ten years younger. Nicole was surprised to note that it was the first genuine smile she'd ever received from him. It warmed her deep inside.

"How about canned stew?"

She hadn't eaten from a can since her college days, but strangely didn't find the idea repulsive. "Sounds good."

Ace poked at the embers from the fire he'd built earlier, then set the opened can on some ash-colored pieces of wood. He dug around in the backpack for a few minutes, then joined her on the rock.

His denim-covered hip rested next to hers. She scooted over as much as possible, but wished she hadn't when she heard Ace's mocking chuckle.

The fire, the star-studded sky and the sounds of night made the atmosphere intimate. And the fact that Ace sat mere inches from her, close enough to see the rise and fall of his chest and close enough to feel the passion emanating from his body made her insides constrict in a way they hadn't since her first high school crush on Kevin Kruise.

Ace stood and stirred the can of stew with a spoon. "Just a few more minutes."

She watched as he moved around the camp fire. The dancing light added to the air of mystery surrounding him. She knew the things about him that he wanted known, but didn't have a clue as to what made Ace bitter. And she wanted to find out.

He glanced over, catching her staring.

"Something wrong, Nicky?"

Self-consciously she wrapped her arms across her chest. "Nothing." To add further to her embarrassment, her voice cracked on the second syllable.

"I have another jacket if you're cold."

"I'm fine, really."

Ace sat on the ground near the fire. "Join me. It's warmer."

Common sense warned her to avoid close contact, then deserted her. Without analyzing why she wanted to be with him, Nicole stood, gingerly placing her weight on her sprained ankle.

He offered his hand for support and she took it, lowering herself to the ground next to him. He held her hand for long seconds, and her gaze for even longer.

The fire crackled, the dying embers emitting heat and encouraging intimacy.

"You look tired."

The way he said it didn't sound like a criticism . . . which made for a surprising change. "I'm exhausted," she admitted. "I could go for a glass of wine and a long soak in a tub, followed by a good night's sleep under a down comforter."

"'Fraid you'll have to settle for a swig of stale water, a damp ground and tomorrow's clothes as a pillow."

"Sounds heavenly."

"Wait 'til you get a load of dinner. Veal parmigiana never tasted so good."

Again, the man was a paradox. Just when she thought she had him pegged as a hotshot, backwoods pilot more at home with thugs than tuxedos, he said something that completely threw her for a loop.

He squatted in front of the fire, and she was ashamed of herself for noticing the way the tight pants molded to his buttocks.

"Ah, perfect. Dinner is served."

Ace grabbed a set of cutlery that was joined together, the kind she hadn't seen since Girl Scouts. He

unhooked them, tossed the knife into the opened backpack, then stood and turned around. Devilish intent
stoked his gaze as he said, "You don't have germs, do
you?"

"What?"

"Germs. You know, nasty little things that shouldn't
be shared."

"Certainly not."

"Didn't think so. Wouldn't have kissed you so thor-
oughly yesterday if I thought you did."

Her heart pounded. He sat down beside her again,
can in hand. Nicole's stomach growled when the tantalizing aroma of food drifted through the air.

After stirring the contents, he drew out a large chunk
of potato smothered with gravy. She hungrily eyed the
meal as Ace closed his lips around the fork.

"One for me," he said. "And one for you."

He returned the fork to the can.

She reached for the utensil.

He shook his head.

Her pulse pounded in her throat. He couldn't possibly be serious. Good heavens above, the man was crass.
With a capital *C*. So why on earth did her stomach
suddenly plunge?

Hormones, she told herself. It was *that* time of the
month.

Lead me not into temptation, she pleaded silently.

She opened her mouth. *And lead me not into acting
in strange ways with an even stranger man.*

Not for any rational reason, her eyelids drifted together as he teased her taste buds with the succulence of
tender meat.

He was so close, she could smell his outdoorsy scent.
So close, she could hear the sharp intake of his breath.

So close, she remembered the way their tongues had met, retreated, then finally danced.

She closed her mouth. Oh, Lord, the fork was still warm from his mouth, still moist from him. Her insides melted.

Hormones.

Try as she might, she couldn't convince herself that it was only wild chemistry doing funny things to her. It was something more, something she dared not name.

She opened her eyes. Ace wore an expression of muted passion. That much she recognized.

By the time they were finished with the meal, Nicole's stomach was so constricted, she couldn't force another bite.

He cleaned up the mess, then threw dirt on the fire. "Ready?"

She glanced at the tiny tent. She knew it was too much to hope that she would get it all to herself. Exhaustion claimed her in the form of lethargy, and she procrastinated. There wouldn't be room to turn over in the tent, and even if she scooted all the way to one side, Ace's body would still dominate her space. And her mind's thoughts.

"Nicole?"

"Ready for what?" Apart from admitting she was afraid to crawl into bed with him, she didn't have any option. And she refused to amuse Ace that way.

He pulled back the flap to the tent. She ducked, trying to avoid touching his arms, or worse, his thighs. But like kids at recess playing London Bridge, his arms fell down and he trapped her against his chest.

"Scared?"

The word wasn't a taunt, but rather a reassurance. "Yes," she admitted, breathless.

"Look at me, Nicole."

Obediently, like a puppet without will or mind, she tipped her head back. The distant glow of the moon's halo glinted from his eyes.

"I'm not hard up."

She had no doubt. He probably had women scattered throughout the world. A woman in every port.

"I want you, Nicky. I think you know that."

She nodded, unable to find her voice.

"But I want you warm and willing. You have nothing to fear from me. I'll keep my hands to myself."

"And your thoughts?"

His chuckle was deeply masculine. With bold appraisal, his gaze swept her, lingering on the thrust of her nipples. "My thoughts, darlin'? Well, they're all mine."

She tried to turn, but he wouldn't release her.

"I'll have you, Nicole."

"Even if it's only to try and get me to change my mind about the island."

"I'd like to change your mind, but believe me, the island has nothing to do with this."

Purposefully, he pulled her against him. She felt his hardness. Nicole gulped, overwhelmed.

"*We* have everything to do with this. You and me. And long, lonely nights."

Desperately she shook her head.

"Just say the word, Nicole, and you shall be mine."

"Never."

His fingers danced down the length of her spine. Her limbs became weak and she trembled. With a single, seductive motion, he'd made a lie of her vow.

"Sleep, Nicky, for tomorrow you walk."

She entered the tent and he dropped the flap. She heard the rasp of metal teeth as he drew the zipper closed.

With him on the outside.

Hell. Pure hell.

She'd died and they'd buried her in a green, weed-choked humidity-drenched grave with flies and mosquitoes. And snakes and lizards. And fireflies the size of hummingbirds.

And the devil was Ace Lawson.

If Nicole thought being confined in a single-passenger Cessna with Ace was unbearable, being alone with him for days and days in the heat was torture.

She'd had it with his constant driving demands that they keep walking. Marco Polo couldn't have followed their trail. With a map and compass.

She was tired, hungry, thirsty and sick of Ace's company. She wanted to go home, relax in a bath topped by bubbles, with a bottle of fine Zinfandel and hours of leisure time to do nothing but indulge.

But that wasn't to be.

When she couldn't walk another foot, he carried her. When she fell into the tent at night exhausted, she couldn't sleep because he wasn't holding her. Then later, when his watch shift was done and he felt sure they were safe, he would climb in beside her. His scent would fill her senses and desire would fill her deep inside. And then she wouldn't sleep because he *was* holding her.

"It's time you earned your keep."

Furious, she looked up at him. Her ankle, though recovering, throbbed from hours of constant use. "Just what in the hell do you mean by that?"

"You've been paying me to protect you, Ms. Jackson, not pamper you. It's time you paid back a little of the overtime I've been putting in."

She swiped her hair back from her forehead. Her stomach jumped at the implication rich in his words and attitude. *It's time you earned your keep.* "But you promised... You said..."

"Dinner, Nicole. Dinner."

"Dinner?" she echoed, with an obvious sigh of relief.

"I'll have soup." With that, he dropped onto the ground.

"You want *me* to make dinner?"

He exhaled from deep in his chest, a long-suffering sound. "It's only fair, I mean, I've cooked every meal for four days now. You can't possibly object."

Dinner. He wanted dinner. Not her. She didn't know whether to laugh or cry.

Ace's conversation was always rich in sexual innuendo. He'd made her hotter and more desperate than the Cabo de Bello sun ever had. And all he was interested in was his stomach.

"Can opener's in the backpack."

In a daze, she scrounged through their diminishing supplies. Her hand closed around the warm metal. She pulled it and a can of soup out. She tried to stab the can with the opener but missed. Frustrated, she tried again.

"Open it, Nicky. Don't kill it."

"I'm trying." On the third attempt, she stabbed her hand. "Damn!"

In an instant, Ace was on his feet and beside her. He took the can from her and put it on the ground. "Nicky?" He uncurled her fingers from the opener, then placed it on top of the can. "What's wrong?"

Despite her best intentions, despite the fact she kept telling herself over and over that she didn't cry, that she hadn't cried since she was sixteen years old and Kevin Kruise invited her best friend to the prom instead of her, Nicole wiped a tear from her eye. Gently Ace took her hand.

With the pad of his thumb, he traced the path of tears that were winding down her cheek. His kindness melted her resistance.

"Nicky?"

She felt miserable. Her feet hurt. New skin had formed over the blisters, but they were still tender. Her ankle twinged when she stood for more than a few minutes. Her brand-new, designer aerobic shoes were mottled brown, the last traces of white leather having disappeared days ago. Her blue jeans made her uncomfortable and she wanted nothing more than a good night's sleep and to freshen up.

But the worst was Ace. He alternated between bullying tyrant and courageous protector.

She wanted to forget the island, her job. She couldn't forget the island, nor her job.

She liked him. She hated him.

She wanted him to stay away.

She wanted him to make love to her.

He drew her closer, and she buried her head in the comfort of the cotton shirt covering his chest. It seemed her life had dramatically changed in only a few days. Gone were the fancy clothes and the supple leather of her shoes. Ace barely gave her time to yank the tangles from her hair each morning. Gone was the routine of one hundred tugs with a brush specially designed to protect the hair shaft from split ends. She'd worn the same jeans two days in a row since she didn't have access to a washer and dryer. Makeup was something she now put on for the sunscreen factor rather than for vanity. She'd even shoved her diamond-studded earrings deep into Ace's duffel bag.

If only her board could see her now . . .

At least, she thanked the gods, her time of the month had come and gone already.

She felt the pressure of Ace's palm against her back. He was urging her closer, until only their clothes separated their hungered touch.

"Talk to me, darlin'."

Nicole shook her head. She knew he wouldn't understand at best, that he would laugh at worst.

His fingertips skimmed the length of her spine.

Reluctantly, she told him. "My hair's a mess."

His reaction was not what she expected. Instead of laughter or taunts about growing up and leaving the big-city glamor behind, she felt him fumbling with the band securing her hair in a thick ponytail.

"There's nothing wrong with your hair."

The band fell to the ground. In the failing light of the setting sun, she allowed him to tip her head back. Shimmering silver danced off his dark blond hair and his eyes contained a glint of something forbidden.

She felt such freedom when he dug his fingers into her hair and combed it out. It fell around her shoulders in waves and drifted across her face.

Ace smoothed back her hair, tucking it behind her ears. "I've been wanting to do that all day."

Her breath caught.

"Next complaint?"

He made it impossible to think. She could only feel. . . .

"Your makeup?" he guessed. "Don't need it, Nicky. Just takes away from your naturalness. The color the sun puts in your face is more alluring than the fake 'primal rose' blush you've been wearing."

"How...?"

"You keep some of your stuff in my bag, darlin'."

"I need a bath," she said.

"Your wish is my command. In the morning."

"Do you mean it?"

"I swear on the Boy Scout oath."

"You were never a Boy Scout."

"But I do know a thing or two about survival. And I know I need this to survive."

He leaned down and captured her lips, demanded her tongue... then her total submission.

"Ace?"

"Hmm?"

"The color is called primrose."

Seven

She could imagine that the intimacy with Ace last night had never really happened.

He'd kissed away the tears, the pain, the frustration.

Then he'd made her prepare dinner, light the fire and pitch the tent. She would have been angry, but there was something about the teasing way in which he'd instructed her in survival fundamentals that made her warm and liquid.

"'Mornin', Nicky."

Nicole paused in midstroke with the comb.

He emerged from the tent, top button of his jeans open. His hair was rumpled and his chest was bare.

He looked seductive, a promise of sin.

"Sleep well?"

She nodded, unable to actually voice the lie. Most of the night she'd lain on her side, faced away from him. She'd stared through the transparent nylon walls. The sounds of his sleep kept her on edge, always expecting him to turn over and claim her lips once more. But he hadn't. And that had been even more frustrating. "And you?"

"Slept like the innocent."

Only she knew he wasn't.

"And dreamed like the wicked."

She felt as though an ice cube—slick from being warmed in his mouth—slid down her back.

He closed the distance between them and compelled her to look at him. She tried, but didn't get past his chest. A mat of hair covered his naked skin, the curls strangely inviting. Her last boyfriend's chest had been bare and she'd never had a desire to run her fingers over the smooth flesh. But heaven help her, she wanted nothing more than to explore the solid, hair-covered part of Ace's anatomy.

Must be the heat, she told herself.

The laces of his shoes were untied, as though he were fully prepared to go back to bed.

"After everything we shared last night, I thought..."

She gulped, then looked up. His eyes were alight with mischief.

"You'd be ready to help with breakfast, darlin'. We seem to have worked up an appetite."

Heat, that had nothing to do with the temperature, climbed up her face.

"Nicole? Don't be shy with me, darlin'. We've been through just about it all."

With that, he disappeared behind a boulder. To stop thinking about him, she busied herself with preparing breakfast. At least yesterday they'd found some fruit to supplement their meal. She was getting tired of eating granola and dried meat. Forget the expensive wines and bubble baths she told herself, she would settle for a cup of coffee, a toilet—whether or not it flushed—and a basin of fresh water.

Odd how she was starting to learn what truly mattered. Her steel-blue Jaguar XJ-S wasn't doing her a heck of a lot of good sitting in a climate-controlled garage.

Ace joined her and accepted the beef jerky without even raising his brow. He was accustomed to roughing it, and actually appeared to like it.

"Thanks."

She'd noticed the difference sometime yesterday afternoon. He'd stopped looking behind them every five minutes, stopped taking constant compass checks. At lunchtime he hadn't been in a hurry to break camp and continue into the bowels of Cabo de Bello. The pace he'd set wasn't as arduous as previous days. He still took care to conceal the campfire, but he wasn't as quick and methodical as he'd been at the beginning of their retreat from reality.

And age wasn't carved as deeply into his features. He'd smiled last night, and then again this morning.

She'd seen touches of a caring man under his devil-may-care attitude. He'd held her while she cried, wiped away her tears, combed her hair. And though they were pitted on opposite sides of a very important issue, had thousands of things that made them diametrical opposites, she'd started to care for him.

"Not hungry this morning?"

She looked at the unopened granola bar.

"You should eat. I've said it before. You'll need your strength."

For what? she wanted to ask. She knew he felt it, too, the attraction that built to a heated pitch whenever they got close.

They broke camp together, working side by side as a team. Another first.

"You're getting good at that," he said, feathering her hair away from her face.

She felt like a child, anxious for approval. A callus on his thumb scraped across her cheek. An instant awareness flooded her.

"Leave your hair loose, Nicky. For me?"

She could have denied him nothing. Even if she wanted to. "If you comb it for me."

His callus arced across her skin again. "Deal."

Several hours later, Ace shucked the backpack from his shoulders. The sun hung overhead, a brilliantly bright, burning ball. Sweat trickled down the inside of her shirt, and she was certain the elastic of her bra was permanently attached to her skin. But the jeans were the worst. It felt as though she'd been melted into them.

"Are we resting?"

"I promised you a bath, remember?"

"I didn't think you were serious."

"Darlin', I never make promises I can't keep."

The words hovered between them.

"Follow me, milady. Your bath awaits."

Giddy, she accepted his hand. She laughed, his infectious grin contagious. Not more than thirty seconds later, he emerged in a clearing. A small lake, its water sparkling and inviting, loomed before her.

"Ace, it's wonderful."

"I'm glad you approve."

A sneaky suspicion dawned on her. "How did you know it was here?"

"Instinct?"

"Try again." She folded her arms across her chest.

"Luck?"

"No one's that lucky, Lawson."

"Isn't it enough to enjoy it?"

"I want answers."

He looked as if he'd been caught with his hand in the proverbial cookie jar. "I saw it two days ago."

"You saw it..." Her voice trailed off into incredulity. "Two days ago? Do you mean to tell me..."

"That we've been walking in circles? 'Fraid so."

Her feet had blistered, the first rough, bumpy skin she'd had in her life. She'd worn the same clothes for more than two days and she'd been deprived of fresh water. Every muscle and sinew, and a few she hadn't known existed, had protested each step, but she'd resolutely kept her mouth shut. While her protector led them on a merry chase around the countryside. In circles. "Ace Lawson, you're a low-down, no-good, despicable animal who doesn't deserve—"

"Hold it, Nicky," he interrupted. He captured her around the shoulders. "It was for your own good. I wanted to make sure we weren't being followed. Two days ago, when I saw the clearing, I wasn't convinced it was safe."

"Give me a break, Mr. Lawson."

"Ah, are we back to that? Look, do you want your cute little tush to arrive back in L.A. in an airplane seat, or doesn't it matter to you if it's in a pine box?"

She sucked in a deep breath. He was right, but the days of walking, the pain of raw feet, the agony of overworked muscles and the sleepless nights conspired to make her irritable.

"Come on, Nicky," he urged, his tone cajoling. "Do you want to swim or would you rather tear into me?"

Like the steam rising from the fertile earth each morning, Nicole's anger evaporated.

A slow smile spread across his masculine features. It started at the corners of his mouth and ended at his eyes, deducting lines and years of what must have been haunting memories. "I'll stand watch while you bathe."

"In your dreams. You'll stand with your back to me."

"That's what I meant."

He lied. They both knew it, but he did it in such a bald-faced manner, she couldn't hold it against him.

"Behind those trees."

"I can't see the other side of the lake from there."

"You can't see the lake, period, if you turned your back like you promised."

He nodded in acknowledgment.

She couldn't help it. She grinned in return.

"You're paying me to protect you," he reminded her.

"Yes, but who's going to protect me from you?"

"Touché, Nicky. Touché."

She saw stark desire in his gaze. The intensity shook her all the way down to her swollen toes.

"Just remember, you, yourself are the only protection you have against me. Tell me 'no' once and you won't have a thing to worry about."

"And if I don't say no?"

"Well, darlin', you'll be in for the flight of your life." His eyes turned darkly serious. "Run hard and fast, Nicole, or don't run at all."

Ace turned and left her in the clearing. Her breaths came in short, belated bursts. Goose bumps prickled her at the thought of joining with Ace. She should heed his advice and run. But even though her brain issued the order, her body refused to comply.

The ice protecting her heart from him was beginning to melt and she felt the effects somewhere deep, somewhere no man had managed to touch.

With unbelievable self-consciousness, she bent down to untie her laces. Her jeans pulled between her thighs uncomfortably. Finally free of shoes and socks, she walked near the lake's edge and squished her toes in the refreshingly cool water.

She eased the shirttails from her waistband. What if Ace watched, though he promised not to? Oh, well, if she wanted a bath, she didn't have much choice. Fingers shaking, she unbuttoned her shirt and allowed it to fall to the ground.

Her jeans were next.

Standing in the shade of palm trees, she hesitated. She was wearing bra and panties, covering a lot more of her anatomy than some swimsuits. "Ace?"

"Yeah?"

The trees and foliage muffled his voice, making it impossible to judge how far away he was.

"Everything okay?" he asked.

"Fine."

Nicole decided to trust Ace's promise. She unhooked the front butterfly on her bra, then wiggled her panties over her hips and down her legs.

She waded into the water, delighted when it washed over her heated body. When the water swirled around her thighs, she decided to slice through it, needing the tension relief from taking a few laps across the short distance.

For the first time in days, she felt gloriously free. She wasn't dripping sweat and she'd managed to shed the dirty clothes.

She suddenly stopped, midstroke.

She hadn't brought fresh clothes with her to the shore. Which only left her two options, dressing in dirty denim or asking Ace for help.

Absently she wondered how long she could stay underwater. For a few minutes, she continued to glide through the water, wetting her hair.

"Hey, Nicky! Want some soap?"

He actually had soap? And he hadn't told her until now? She knew the oversight wasn't accidental.

"I'll bring it down without looking."

"I'll bet," she muttered.

"What?" he called.

"Leave it on the shore. Would you bring me a change of clothes, too?"

"Sure thing."

She found the deepest part of the lake and treaded water, hoping it would shade her body from his view.

It took him a whole lot less time than she imagined it should to reach the shore. Just how close had he been?

Nicole made a tent with her hands and placed them near the top of the water, hoping the shield blocked his view. He didn't even look in her direction.

Instead, he whistled while he put down the items. Then he was gone and she found his chivalry chafed. She raced for the shore.

The soap was there, along with jeans and shirt. And fresh bra. And no panties. Was there to be no end to her mortification? He could have brought her duffel.

Nicole unwrapped the small bar of soap that looked as if it had been taken from a cheap hotel. The scent of the bar wasn't even particularly inspiring, but it would freshen her.

Twenty or thirty minutes later, the soap had been lathered until only a sliver remained. She should have saved him some, but she'd needed a lot to wash her hair. She emerged from the lake, feeling like a new person.

"Five minutes, and I'm coming in."

She hurried.

Brushing the water from her body, she slid her arms between the straps of her bra . . . the bra warmed by the sun, touched by Ace's masculine fingers.

She pulled on her shirt, rolled up the sleeves, then reached for the pants. She was shocked by their length. Judging by the ragged, frayed edges, Ace had obviously taken his killer knife to the material and sliced it off right below the pockets. Dismay welled inside her. Though she appreciated the thought and knew she would be less likely to suffer from the heat, he'd made them too short. The length would hardly cover her bare buttocks. But then, he'd probably intended it that way.

Having no other choice, she tugged them on. As she suspected, they covered enough, and nothing more. And she'd never felt so free. Damn him.

"Are you done yet?"

"Yes."

Seconds later he emerged from the trees.

She was suddenly very conscious of the length of the shorts. The breeze stirred against her legs, her bare legs.

Ace whistled. Long and low. She pulled at the back of the shorts, trying to make sure it didn't creep any higher.

"Don't," he instructed. "They're fine. Great."

She surprised herself by not reacting negatively to his masculine approval. In fact, a small corner of her heart welcomed the appreciation. She hadn't dated in a couple of years, the daily grind of running a corporation taking most of her time and all of her energy. If she watered her plants once a week, she felt decadent.

Out in the middle of godforsaken Cabo de Bello, she was learning things about herself. Like the fact that cellular technology wasn't terribly important.

But the hungry stare of a predatory male was enough to ignite her already-stoking desire and make her forget that a world outside of their reality existed . . . a reality she knew would crumble around her soon. Too soon.

Ace pulled open the snap of his jeans. The sound reverberated. The rasp of a yielding zipper was next, followed by the deliberate tug on the hem of his shirt.

Nicole gathered her dirty clothes and turned away.

"Thought you might want to wash those in the lake."

"I do. I will . . . when you're finished."

She heard a splash and instinctively looked. Fortunately—she pushed aside the part of her that whispered, "Unfortunately"—the water covered past his hips.

"We've earned a little R and R. We'll stay here the rest of the day."

Elation rushed through her. At least twelve hours to rest her feet. Time to sit and enjoy the scenery, watch the sun's beams give way to the moon's rays.

Time to be alone with Ace without bone-weary exhaustion separating them.

Another sensation rushed into the place of elation. Her heart did triple time.

Nicole hurried back through the trees, away from her companion. While she frolicked in the water, he'd been busy. A tent stood, its angles in perfect symmetry. Rocks had been arranged in a circle for a fire, and he'd gathered wood.

She was sitting on the ground, cross-legged, and pulling a brush through her hair when he returned.

"I promised to do that," he said.

Excitement tingled inside. No one had brushed her hair since elementary school when the girls all took turns combing each other's hair while they were supposed to be watching movies about the life habits of baboons.

Their fingers mated as she passed off the brush to Ace.

He positioned himself behind her, legs spread wide, all but straddling his pelvis against her back. She kept her spine stiff, not willing to give in to the gentle tugs and allowing herself to curve into his hardness.

Her eyes drifted shut and she relaxed for the first time in days. His touch felt good, the heat didn't feel as intense, the humidity not nearly as drowning.

Los Angeles seemed so far away. Even the island politics faded into obscurity. All that existed were the gentle sounds of nature, the sensations of sensuality as Ace continued to stroke the brush through her hair.

"What're you thinking, Nicky?"

"That I like it when you do that."

"Ah." He started at her scalp, the bristles massaging her head. "What else would you like me to do for you?"

She tried to answer, but couldn't even force herself to speak.

"Hmm, Nicky?"

He stretched out the *Y,* as if it were a caress.

"I have a few suggestions," he murmured against her cheek.

She smelled his freshness, felt the warmth from his breath. Resistance pooled. She curved against Ace.

The brush stopped.

Behind her back, his chest was solid. Through the softness of her shirt, the roughness of the hairs on his bare chest tantalized her. Heaven help her, rational thought had fled on wings more sure and swift than those of his twin-seater Cessna.

Suddenly she wished the three remaining days were weeks longer. The enforced isolation appealed to her on a primitive level. Even the bugs weren't bugging her.

"First suggestion." Ace's fingers found her shoulders. With expert manipulation, he massaged the flesh, working out tension and the kinks of half a week's trials.

"Relax, darlin'...enjoy."

Her head dropped forward, hair framing her face. He outlined her shoulder blades with gentle, but steady pressure, pressing just hard enough that she felt her energy ebb. She wouldn't move now if someone paid her to.

He pushed aside the remaining strands of hair from her neck and shoulders. Using only his thumbs, he started tracing her spine all the way from the base of her skull to the grooved hollow where her back melded into womanly curves.

Not just from the unusual position, her breaths came in small, irregular spurts. His touch excited her, made her long, made her want and yearn, all at the same, intoxicating time. He moved closer; she felt his swollen hardness press against her.

The day would end in lovemaking, of that she had no doubt. And she had even less desire to deny him, despite their differences, despite the fact she might never see him again after the end of the week, despite the fact her one goal in life drove an insurmountable wall between them.

His kiss at the sensitive part of her spine made her stomach melt. He turned seduction into an art, reduced her to clay to be molded, sculpted...be made his.

"I want you, Nicky."

"I know," she said softly.

The chirps of the birds high in the trees spoke more loudly than Ace. Still, he continued his ministrations.

"I want you, darlin', I want your honesty, I want your uninhibited response. Tell me to stop, Nicky. Tell me to stop if you don't want it as much as I do. Be honest, darlin', but tell me now, before I *can't* stop."

Eyes opened wide, she turned in his arms. Crouched in front of him, she took a steadying breath, not believing her own actions, and said, "Don't stop, Ace."

"Ah, Nicky..."

With his hands, he cradled her face. She felt safe, as if nothing and no one could harm her. After so many years of being in control, always fighting her way to the top, the feeling was new...and not unwelcome. She had the odd feeling, though, that if she clashed against Ace in a corporate boardroom, she might lose the battle.

"Open your mouth for me, darlin'. Let me taste you."

She did so, willingly.

He drew closer slowly, an agonizing slowness that set her nerve endings aflame.

His tongue found hers. She responded tentatively, the tip of his tongue shooting darts of pleasure low in her body, until she felt butterflies flutter to life.

He stroked her cheekbones with his thumbs in a way that was both proprietary and coaxing. Nicole didn't doubt she belonged with him. To him. She groaned softly and he swallowed the sound of pleasure.

Trepidation raced through her when he reached for the top button on her shirt.

"Relax, darlin'," he said, kissing her soundly again before working the button through its tiny hole. "I'll go slow. I won't hurt you." His hand trembled. "And I swear I'll make this as good for you as I can."

She nodded.

In seconds, her buttons surrendered.

Ace scooted back a few inches. "I want to see you."

Nicole pulled her lip between her teeth. The request unnerved her, in the middle of the day, in the open wilderness. It was strange, a little intimidating. And exciting in its forbiddenness.

He pushed the shirt from her shoulders, letting the garment slide down her back and over her hands. He swept the expensive linen from the dirt, folded it carelessly, then shoved it into the backpack. She was grateful he hadn't allowed her last clean shirt to trail across the earth, grateful he'd taken the time to think of doing the small favor, for she was already beyond rational thought.

His gaze was unashamedly hungry as he spanned his hands across her spine and pulled her closer.

She felt no shyness when his head lowered and he fumbled with the front clasp on her bra. Gently he cupped her breasts in the palms of his hands. His fingers closed around the now-tender weight of her breasts and Nicole felt her eyelids drift together.

The birds sang, and the sun's light streamed through the palm tree fronds, warming her skin. Nicole instinctively knew the simmering in her loins was caused by Ace, not the tropics.

He kissed the pulse pounding in her throat. Tension drained. When Ace started to move his hands so that he rolled each nipple between a thumb and forefinger, a breath gushed from deep inside.

He squeezed her nipples in a motion that was equal measures pleasure and pain. She wanted more. Nicole whispered his name and was rewarded when he took the swollen tip in his mouth, caressing it with his teeth.

She'd never known such ecstasy. Her last short-term relationship had consisted of a quick dive between the sheets before both of them passed out. Neither she nor her partner had ever gotten creative, nor explored each other, as much from lack of time as lack of energy.

But she knew already that Ace was going to be a demanding lover. He wouldn't be satisfied with once a week, assuming no other commitments came along, and she doubted he would accept the headache excuse.

He swirled his tongue around her nipple, coaxing even more response from her. She didn't think it was possible to be more aroused, until he gently bit the tip.

She sagged forward.

"Easy, darlin'," he said while continuing to stimulate her other breast.

"Ace?"

"Hmm?"

"I don't..." She trailed off, trying to remember what had been so important. Sensation after sensation swept over her. Her body began to move in time with his coaxing, his suckling. "It ..."

"What, Nicky? It what? I want your honesty. Can you be honest? For me? For us?"

She felt the climax begin to build in the pit of her womanliness. She didn't want it, not yet. It was too soon. Ace hadn't even undressed—he wasn't receiving any of the pleasure he gave. She felt selfish. "Stop." The word emerged as a sexy husk. "I think I'm going, going to..." Embarrassment clawed at her. How could she possibly tell him he'd aroused her so much, she was near to going over the edge?

"Does it feel good, darlin'?"

"Ah." She gasped. "Ace!"

"Is that a yes?"

"Cr-crass," she managed. "You're crass."

"I've been called worse." He chuckled. "Do you like it?" He froze. "You still want me to stop? I don't want to, Nicky. I want it to be special for you. I want you to enjoy."

He gave an example.

"Don't stop."

The sound he made was triumphant. She began to quake, and still he kept teasing, tasting.

The feeling built to a crescendo pitch. Between her legs, her shorts damped with the heat of her own need. When she thought she was going to explode, he stopped.

In a frustrated whoosh, her breath escaped.

Before she could catch it again, he'd moved his mouth to her other nipple.

If he'd encouraged a climax earlier, he now demanded it.

Embarrassment fled.

He took her to the edge of the precipice. Resistance, thoughts of why things couldn't work between them, all the logical reasons she shouldn't make love with Ace, all the things that made them diametrical opposites vanished from thought. Under his touch, his sexily whispered words, she felt. She experienced.

And then she slid over the edge.

Eight

Ace captured her moan with his lips.

He'd demanded she be honest with herself. And she had been. So honest, it shook him down to the core. So honest, he didn't know if he could return the same.

Nicole's head dropped back. Her lips were reddened from passion, her eyelids partially shading the vibrant green color of her eyes. She looked beautiful.

She bore his mark of love.

Of possession.

Of belonging.

To him.

Ace reached to smooth the tangled strands of hair away from her face. His breath stuck in his chest. She was his, but he knew it wouldn't last.

In three days, and if he were lucky, three nights, they'd have to return to civilization. Cabo de Bello's political infrastructure had been unstable lately. But if his hunch was right, the rebels had already been subdued. In fact, their tenuous power had probably lasted less than seventy-two hours. If he'd been alone, he would have stayed with the Maldanados and taken his chances. But he was being paid to safeguard Nicole's tush—cute as it was—and hadn't been willing to risk her hide. Seventy-two hours wasn't long in the scheme of things, but long enough for lives to be lost.

Nicole's eyes slowly opened. She smiled shyly.

He smiled in return. "You okay?" he asked. He admitted her answer mattered. As much as he said he would manipulate her if it helped him win, he realized it had gone past that. He couldn't do it. Their lovemaking would be open, not hidden by secret agendas.

"Fine. How about you?"

"Hurting like hell."

Shyness seemed to return to Nicole with his bald statement. A blush crept up her cheekbones, highlighted over the tan she'd acquired traveling under the southern sun. She reached for the backpack. For her shirt?

"Don't," he said, capturing her wrist. "I like to look at you."

"But—"

"No buts, Nicole. You're a beautiful woman with a gorgeous body. I enjoy looking at you." Using the hold he had on her, he pulled her closer. "And I enjoy touching you even more."

He spanned his free hand across her back, then slowly moved to the front, tracing along the bottom of her ribs. He watched her breathing change, saw the pulse pound in her throat. Her flush of self-consciousness faded, and her lips parted.

As he gently closed around her breast, he was again struck by the total honesty of her arousal. Nicole Jackson may fight him on everything, including the color of the sky, but in his arms, she responded completely.

He had to possess her, soon, or he would go crazy with the wanting.

He stood, then helped her to her feet. Ace swept her into his arms, managed to grab the backpack on the second swipe, then fumbled with the tent's flap. He cursed savagely, an inferno building inside with each second he delayed.

His body was tired of being magnanimous.

The hard ground was not what he wanted for her. Satin sheets, champagne and caviar were more her style. He easily pictured her wearing a silk teddy, freshly washed hair gleaming as it reflected the light from a hundred flickering candles.

And all he had to offer was a dingy sleeping bag.

He placed her on it and reality surpassed the mental image. Silk and satin be damned, she was the most sensational woman he'd ever been with. And he knew he wanted her more than he'd ever wanted a woman.

Ace reached for the snap securing her shorts around her waist.

She placed her hand on his. "You first."

For a second, he wished he hadn't demanded her honesty. The raw sensuality in her gaze hit him like a chop to the jaw.

With uncharacteristic impatience, he leaned over to unfasten his shoes. He tugged off one, then hopped on the bare foot while he tried to work the knot out of the second lace.

Nicole laughed at him. Hell. Even the sound of her voice sent seductive thoughts through his mind. And lower.

Barefoot, he pulled his jeans zipper down, wincing when the metal abraded his swollen need. He pushed the material past his hips, then frowned when he saw her eyes open wide.

"You don't have underwear on."

"Don't wear 'em."

"Never?" she asked.

"Never."

"I see."

"So I see."

She looked away, as though trying not to be caught staring.

Problem was, he liked the way she looked at him.

Ace knelt near her. "Allow me." Using his thumb, he pried apart the snap at her waistband. With a slowness meant to torture her, but in reality tortured him far more, he pulled the zipper down. She lifted her hips to allow him to tug the material down her thighs.

He exposed her belly button, and groaned.

How much could he endure?

He tugged again, then swore softly. "You're not wearing underwear, either."

"You didn't bring me any."

"Ahh. Right. Holy—"

His body responded instantly. If he didn't go mad before he bedded her, he would be surprised. Quickly he shoved aside the material.

He covered her with his body, then felt her tense, her knees lock as he tried to move between her soft thighs. Idiot. He felt as inept as a teen in the back seat of a Chevy.

Ace pushed away from her, then raked a hand through his hair.

"Sorry." Her voice emerged as a whisper.

"Don't be," he said. "My fault."

"I'm just..."

"Go on."

She flushed, though she made no attempt to hide herself. "It's been a while, and—"

"Say no more," he said. Hell, he knew well enough what it was like to go without for long periods of time. Business had been good, and he'd had the opportunity to fly more mercy missions in the past six months than he had in the previous two years. Which meant his last stop in Cartagena had been months ago, maybe even half a lifetime ago.

Nicole was nervous.

He gulped a little masculine pride.

So was he.

Too bad another part of his anatomy was anxious to get the show on the road.

What he wouldn't give for candlelight and wine right now. Instead, he had sunshine and bugs. Oh, well, improvising was his specialty.

He lay next to her, then pulled her into the crook of his arm. Their calves met, as did their thighs and hips.

Gently he placed a kiss on her forehead. She snuggled closer. With slow, elongated motions, not betraying the tension gnawing in his gut, he began a lazy exploration of her body's secrets.

He learned there were many.

She turned on her side, offering more of herself. Ace shifted, so that his mouth closed around a nipple, while his hand explored the secrets of her femininity. Nicole moaned softly against his shoulder, and a feeling he'd never before experienced stirred somewhere deep. He hesitated before naming it. Tenderness? Ace shrugged it away. It wasn't possible. He'd hardened his heart the day his wife walked out and he swore he wouldn't succumb to womanly wiles again. So he couldn't possibly be letting down his defenses for Nicky.

She sighed softly and her warm breath stirred against his chest. Lord, it felt wonderful to hold her.

Nicole smoothed her hand across his stomach, then higher. Though he didn't know it possible, she rolled one of his nipples between her fingers, just the way he'd done to her. His loins tightened. His breath nearly strangled him.

No woman had aroused him like Nicole did.

He told himself it didn't matter. Told himself he could let her go in a few days, after he won their battle. So why couldn't he convince himself?

Beneath his hand, where he'd parted her to explore the tiny, hidden nub of her center, he felt her grow damp. Her special scent filled the air and her body rocked in time with his motions.

Nicole's touch strayed lower, and her fingernail scratched his stomach. "Go ahead," he said, the words husky. "Touch me."

She took him in her palm and blood surged in his temples.

"Better . . . stop," he said, grabbing her wrist and immobilizing her.

She chuckled, and he was amazed how self-confident she sounded, as if she drew power from her own boldness.

In a quick, efficient motion, he turned, pinning her under him. "Nicole." He wiped traces of sweat from his brow. "Nicky, tell me you need it as much as I do."

"Yes, Ace."

"Not scared?"

"Not anymore."

Though loath to, Ace left her for a second, long enough to dig for a necessary package somewhere in the bottom of the backpack.

"Always ready for an emergency, Lawson?"

"And a few other things, darlin'." Ace had trouble thinking straight. He offered a quick thanks he didn't need to fly tonight, then added a "Damn" when the package slipped from his suddenly too-big fingers.

He'd definitely done better in a Chevy.

Finally he dropped the empty wrapper on the floor, and slipped the condom into place. He returned to Nicole's arms and claimed her mouth with a kiss.

Her tongue met his, thrust for thrust. He tasted her sweetness and it only whetted his appetite for more.

"Ace?"

"Hmm?"

"I'm ready."

"Yeah, darlin'?"

"Now."

He didn't wait for a second invitation.

He sank into her. Nicole's body, warm and wet, welcomed him. She tightened around him, urging him deeper, tempting him with seduction.

He tried to hold still to allow her to adjust, but she started to move in a rhythmic, ancient way that made him tighten and try to hold off at least a few seconds longer than total humiliation. He stroked.

She sighed, thrusting her hips higher.

"Nicky," he warned.

"It's okay," she said, the word a whisper on the air. "Take me later. You go now."

Her statement, so unselfish, moved him. In her own way, Nicole gave more than anyone he knew. She was special, unique. And he only had three more days to explore the depths he was only now beginning to fathom existed.

He felt a throb build, demanding release. His breathing labored. Nicole threaded her arms around his neck, pulled him down, then kissed him.

He didn't stand a chance.

A few seconds later, exhausted, spent, he dropped to his elbows.

"Relax," she said.

"I'm too big."

"Not quite."

He'd get her for that later, he promised himself. As soon as he was able. Carefully, he allowed himself to relax. Nicole drew large circles on his back with a fingernail, the motion feeling sexy, and more, at the same time.

He didn't know how much time they'd wasted, but knew it had to have been significant when he noticed the sun's rays through the tent's walls had dropped and didn't burn as bright as they had earlier.

With a tenderness he didn't know he was capable of, he turned on his side and held Nicole close. Odd, the woman who acted more assured and self-confident than any woman he'd ever known was the first to arouse such intense feelings of protectiveness in him.

Her stomach rumbled, and he realized how long it had been since they'd last eaten. "Hungry?" he asked.

She nodded. "But I'm too lazy to get up and eat."

"It's not laziness, it's satisfaction."

"So you say."

Nicole wiggled against him. Unbelievably, he responded. "What?" he demanded, capturing her earlobe between his lips and then circling her tender flesh with his tongue. "You're not satisfied yet?"

She laughed softly as he tickled her ribs.

"Then we'll have to remedy that situation."

"What are you doing?" she asked with a gasp.

"Making sure you don't have any complaints." Ace shifted so that his tongue traced a warm path down her gently rounded stomach. With the tip of his tongue, he plunged into her navel, while caressing her between her thighs with the other hand.

"Ace!"

"Hmm?" He looked up, noticing that the rough growth of beard on his chin reddened her sensitive skin. "Like it?"

"I. That is . . ."

"Go on."

"Too much."

He grinned. "No complaints, darlin'?"

Her response was lost within a soft whimper.

It wasn't until after he was certain she'd found her release that he took his own for a second time. Where she was concerned, he was insatiable. Three days couldn't possibly be long enough. Hell, a lifetime would be too short.

With a shudder, he lay next to her, their sweat-slick bodies entwined in the way only lovers knew. As his breathing returned to normal, he wondered where thoughts of spending more than three days with Nicole came from.

They were as opposite as polar extremes. Her career and the drive to succeed were her devotion; flying and making medical deliveries were his. Though she hadn't complained as much as he expected about being in the sun and humidity with bugs and reptiles, it wasn't the way she would want to live. And except for occasional stops at his rickety headquarters, Ace spent his life in the air and on the ground, but rarely in a hotel. He hadn't had any place other than his office to call home in years. Until now, he hadn't wanted anywhere to put down roots.

When he got too old for flying and living in tents and sleeping bags, he intended to buy a piece of property somewhere palm trees grew. The only requirement was that the land had to be cheap, because God knew, Ace definitely didn't have money. And after seeing the way money destroyed his life, he had no desire to possess the commodity, which was why he spent every cent he earned on medical supplies.

Nope. As far as a relationship with Nicole was concerned—a relationship with any woman—impossibility compounded impossibility. There was no sense looking beyond the end of the week.

And yet...

Hopefully, things would have cooled politically. He could refuel Cessie and fly into the blue yonder, drop his young female executive back in L.A., then return to Central America with the shipment so desperately needed. Like always, he'd look to the future, and not back at the might-have-beens, if-onlys.

But for now... Ace tugged on his jeans.

"Where are you going?" Nicole asked around a yawn.

Even the way her mouth formed around the motion had the power to pique his interest. "Thought you were hungry."

"I am. I think."

"I'll fix dinner."

"Instant food. I love it."

"Hey, don't complain. We're not down to eating the local vermin. Yet."

She shuddered. He laughed.

"How about pasta?"

"Is there Italian bread with it?"

"'Fraid not."

"Oh, well, I can dream."

"So can we all, darlin', so can we all."

Since he'd picked her up in California, he'd done plenty of that. "Stay there," he said. "I'll be back in a few."

The sun had set by the time he sliced open the packages of instant food. He smelled the artificial flavorings and couldn't work up much enthusiasm. Maybe he'd stay in the U.S. long enough to find a piece of prime rib. The life he'd chosen had hundreds of advantages, but on a rare occasion he missed his penthouse apartment and five-star restaurants. But he didn't miss them enough to consider changing his life-style.

Ace loved the open sky above him, the roll of hills and valleys below him. And if people were dependent on him, that was all right, he lived for the payoff of seeing a sick kid get well. Transporting needed supplies was worth the risks, more so than going to a hundred corporate cut-throat parties a year where everyone pretended.

He returned to the tent. To Nicole.

Her hair hung alluringly messy, erotically tempting. She'd pulled one of his shirts over her bare body, shielding everything but her thighs and arms. Mentally, he pictured the rest.

"Thanks," she said, taking the opened meal from him. She took a bite. "What is this?"

"Linguine." He read the label to be sure. "At least that's what it's supposed to be." He sat next to her. When she crossed her legs yoga-style, he noticed she still didn't have panties on. He stabbed a fork into the silver pouch.

"It's not bad," Nicole said.

"You can say that again."

"I said..." She trailed off as she followed Ace's gaze. "Oh."

They ate in silence, Ace having a difficult time swallowing.

When dinner was finished, Ace cleaned up the mess. The moon replaced the sun, the drone of insects replaced the chirp of birds. Ace felt unusually restless, in need of activity. He knew it didn't come from being followed. Instinct told him they'd never had anyone on their tail. But still, something gnawed him. Something he didn't want to name. "How about a swim?"

"But it's dark."

"So?"

"I don't have a swimsuit."

"You don't need one."

Dawning recognition appeared on her features. But instead of blushing, she smiled. Ace returned the grin. Wanting to be with Nicole was fast becoming a habit.

She accepted his hand up. Though she wasn't petite, he was surprised by how small her hand was inside his. She gave the impression of being strong, capable, infallible. But he'd seen otherwise. She hadn't complained when he'd pushed her to the edge of her endurance. Yet he'd seen the sheen of tears covering her eyes when he'd doctored her blisters. He'd seen her draw her lower lip between her teeth so she didn't cry out when he peeled socks from her shredded skin.

And everything he'd seen made him respect her, melted a part of his heart encased in coldness, made him consider that there were possibilities.

She held his hand while they walked, without benefit of light, toward the water's edge. In the shadowed peeks of moonglow, he noticed her fingers trembled as she bared her body to him.

He dragged in a lungful of air.

He placed his thumbs beneath her chin and tipped her head back. A strange feeling of possessiveness surged through him. The feeling was as unwelcome as it was surprising. Nicole Jackson represented everything he distrusted, the things he purposely chose to avoid. So why was he acting like an insatiable rooster?

Maybe because he felt like one.

He bent his head, and felt her rise on her toes to meet him. Her lips claimed his, an act that teased him. He suppressed the hunger burning inside to deepen the kiss, to ignite the passion flaring inside. She'd initiated the touch, and he wanted her to take the lead.

Hesitantly, then with growing assurance, she slipped her tongue inside his mouth. Ace groaned, then stiffened when her bare chest met his.

Her nipples were taut, tantalizing.

He circled her with his arms, one hand holding her at the base of her neck, the other hand splayed across the roundness of her buttocks.

Powerfully, her tongue delved into his mouth, exploring, demanding the same kind of surrender from him that he'd demanded from her.

He gave. Willingly.

The area between his thighs grew hot and heavy. The urge to protect and penetrate pounded in his loins. He needed her. Again. And again.

With jerky motions, more fit for a teen than a man, he pushed her away, groaning when their bodies lost contact. He swore when hair caught in the zipper of his jeans, then again when the metal teeth tore against him.

He dug around the bottom of the backpack, disgusted when his fingers felt like thumbs. Finally he found what he searched for. Seconds later, protection in place, he lifted her in his arms.

Using instinct as a primal guide, he carried her to the water. "Wrap your arms around my neck."

She did and he felt the ripple of tension that passed through her.

"I'll make it good," he promised.

"I know."

Her tone contained trust, total trust—a change from the beginning of the trip. The responsibility felt awesome.

He waded into the water; the night coolness swirled around his calves, then his thighs. Against his chest, she felt warm. Her hair feathered across him, erotically. Invitingly.

The moon appeared for a flash of a second and he saw into her eyes. Pure passion radiated there. He felt slammed in the solar plexus. Despite the vastness of the world separating them, the impossibility of anything more than shared intimacy, they communicated. They communicated the need for human companionship, though both attempted to verbally deny it.

"I want you, Ace."

He slid her down his body, holding her close.

She shivered. "The water's colder than I thought."

"I'll warm you up."

"I hoped you'd say that."

Using the water's natural buoyancy, he lifted her, setting her on top of him. She took each inch, forming herself around his shaft as if made for that purpose. She felt so good. And he knew there was nothing casual about the way he and Nicole made love. She filled a void in his life. In the morning, he wanted to wake with her in his arms, not drop a twenty on the table before the spread of dawn.

For a second, as she moved up and down on him, he allowed himself to imagine what it would be like to have her with him always. Never dull. Challenging. Exciting. But then his climax began to build and he dismissed the thoughts of happily-ever-after as nothing more than a trick of a sultry night under a brilliant Caribbean moon. They were as different as a windswept moor and a rolling valley. Yet the moment was theirs, even though the future belonged to no one.

But still, the dream spun a soft web around him.

She uttered a soft, seductive sound in his ear. "Ace?"

Knowing she'd reached the same state of insanity as he, he wrapped his arms firmly around her and surged up in a single thrust.

She cried out, her head tipping back, her breasts exposed to the night.

The sight of her, the sounds of her, drove him to his own climax, the release a burst of energy from his deepest parts.

Nine

Nicole became aware of several sensations simultaneously. The sun beat through the tent's walls, warming her, the birds sang a noisy melody, her body felt alive and tingly.

The air hung heavy with humidity; drawing a breath filled her lungs with moisture.

She lay still, not wanting to disturb Ace after the night they'd shared. Her mouth curved into a smile. The man needed his rest.

His palm curved around her breast. Awareness flooded her. She desired him as she'd desired no other man. As sleep still clogged her mind, she wondered why. Why did the one man who made her feel like a woman, have to be the one man with whom it wouldn't be possible to have a future?

They were from opposite sides of the spectrum. If she

was light, he was dark. She couldn't survive in his world; he wouldn't try to survive in hers.

In two more days, their brief fling would end.

Sadness grabbed her.

Must be the tropics, she told herself. Ordinarily, a man like Ace Lawson wouldn't appeal to her. The few men she'd dated were business associates, as hungry to claw their way to the top as she. They understood.

He shifted in his sleep, pulling her closer. His maleness swelled against her buttocks and answering need swirled through her stomach. Even unconscious, he exuded strength and passion. Instinctively, she responded to it.

And just as instinctively, she regretted the fact their time together would be severed. She would never see him again. She wondered why the thought hurt so much. After all, they'd only slept together. Nothing more.

By midday, Nicole knew she was fooling herself.

Ace had awoken, made sweet, sexy love to her, then led her to the lake where they'd taken turns washing each other, lazily exploring each other's bodies. And enjoying each second of it. She'd learned where he was ticklish. And he'd discovered how to bring her to the edge of desire in less than three minutes... without using his hands.

If she thought that once she left Cabo de Bello she could pretend all she and Ace had shared was sex, she suddenly realized she was wrong.

Over the course of the past few days, she'd seen a side of him she wouldn't have suspected was there. No matter what happened, he made certain she was taken care of.

Feminine intuition told her he'd gone above and beyond the call of duty.

And she loved him for it.

"You okay?"

She looked up from where she was sitting to see Ace standing near, an odd expression on his face. She gulped deeply. "Fine, thanks," she lied. Fine didn't describe what she was feeling at all. Weak, delirious, idiotic... They described what she was feeling.

How on earth could she have allowed herself to fall for the tall, rugged pilot? She knew it would mean heartbreak. So why couldn't she have been more intelligent?

"You're flushed."

He walked over to her, shoes crunching the fallen leaves and twigs.

"Must be the heat."

He crouched next to her, and she felt her face grow redder. His hand on her forehead felt wonderfully soothing, relaxing. Forbidden.

She wasn't the type for a one-night stand, and couldn't believe she'd actually slept with Ace, invited him to make love to her. *Must be the tropics,* she told herself again. Another lie.

"You sure you're okay?"

"Positive." She'd always prized honesty. And she was learning to lie like the best of them.

He was so close, she identified his scent. Raw maleness.

"No regrets, darlin'?"

She forced herself to be honest. She wrapped her arms around her knees, then squared her shoulders. "No regrets."

He smiled, a roguish, endearing motion.

Come what may, she had memories. She wouldn't allow after-the-fact thoughts to taint the remembrances.

They ate in silence. By unspoken accord, Nicole spent a few minutes clearing up the mess since Ace had prepared lunch. They were making quite a team.

Restlessness stirred inside her. She wanted Ace. She wanted him to stay away. She wanted him to take her in his arms. She wanted him to leave her alone in order to salvage whatever part of her heart she could.

She cared for him. She wanted *not* to care for him. He had a way of slicing through her defenses, seeing exactly what she didn't want him to see. The way he did it left her feeling naked, emotionally stripped. Vulnerable. Womanly. All the things she'd fought since she'd entered the male-dominated world of corporate America.

Nicole stared at the overcast sky. The atmosphere matched her feelings. Clouds swirled together, dancing around each other, trying to control each other.

"Looks like rain."

She nodded.

"Want to give me a hand digging some trenches and making sure the tent's secure?"

Anything to vent the frustration inside. She stood and took a small shovel from Ace. "Where should I start?"

Above them, she felt the shift in pressure. It was almost as if the heavens responded to her turmoil with turmoil of their own. As she sank the shovel into the ground, the sun disappeared behind a band of ominously gray clouds and the ground felt as though it absorbed an electrical charge.

She looked at Ace and that same current flowed between them.

"Hurry," he called.

With vigor, she plunged in the shovel, then winced in disgust when seeing she'd sliced a worm in half.

"Keep digging," Ace commanded.

Instead of giving him a dirty look as she would have done days ago, she attacked the ground again. If he was urging her, he had good reason. Without an explanation, she trusted him. Another step in the direction of becoming a spellbound bimbo. Oh, well, it would only be for another two days. Then she could resume life as normal.

"You're doing great, darlin'!" he called over the wind, which had picked up.

She ignored the inner feeling that told her after spending a week in the wilds with Ace that nothing would ever be the same again.

Moments later, he was beside her. "Get in the tent. I've already put the food and bags in there."

The wind whipped strands of her loose hair across her face. "What about you?"

"I'll finish the trenches, then I'll join you."

"Hurry." A huge drop of rain pelted her.

He gave her a brief, but blissful kiss. "I will."

The rain dropped down in a torrent. Cabo de Bello never did things by halves on this part of the island, she decided. It was either ninety degrees with ninety percent humidity or it was raining with an intensity to give Noah pause.

Ace returned to the tent ten minutes later, hair plastered to his forehead, and drops of water running from his clothes.

"I like skinny-dipping a lot more than that," he said, shucking his shirt. "Give me a hand with the boots, will you?"

He pushed aside the sleeping bag, then sat on the floor. She knelt in front of him to take his right foot. Nicole pulled. And pulled.

"What did you do, cement them on?"

"Feels like it. Pull harder."

She tried again. And ended on her rear. "Don't you dare laugh."

"Wouldn't dream of it." The gleam in his eyes betrayed him. The corner of his mouth twitched.

Soon she grinned, then laughed. She couldn't help it. Ace's moods were contagious.

It took nearly three minutes to get his boots off; by then, goose bumps had risen on his damp flesh.

"I'll help you get rid of the chill," she said, pushing away the nagging conscience telling her not to get in deeper. The rational part of her recognized it was already too late. The damage had been done. She was hooked.

He cocked an eyebrow. "Is that an invitation?"

"It is."

"Say no more."

She didn't....

An hour later, the sun, submerged by nature, broke free, and unleashed its warming rays on the saturated ground.

She lay, snuggled and content against Ace's chest. The steady rhythm of his beating heart felt intoxicating, telepathing a unique oneness.

"So what exactly is a nice lady like you doing in a place like this?"

Relaxed, she yawned and stretched. Ace had said they should give the earth time to dry a little before venturing outside. She'd agreed and together they'd fallen asleep. She felt completely decadent, taking a nap in the middle of the afternoon. Maybe there was more to life than power lunches and corporate politics.

"Nicky?"

"Do we have to talk about business right now?"

"You have something else in mind?"

She ran her foot up his calf.

"I'm not made of steel, lady."

She propped herself on an elbow. "I'm glad. I like flesh and blood better."

"Get your little butt over here."

She wiggled back into his hold.

"You never answered my question."

"That's because I don't want to think of the office right now."

"It won't go away. We have to go back in two days. A lot could happen in a week."

It had. In less than a week, a man she disliked on sight had become a part of her. And reality felt light-years away. Yet it would catch up to them in less than forty-eight hours.

"Nicole, talk to me."

She sighed. Ace was persistent. That was the quality that made him an excellent pilot, one of the best people in the world at getting others in and out of risky places. "I know how you feel about the plan. We usually end up arguing the point—"

"No arguments." He held up a hand in mock surrender. "I'd like to *talk*, really talk."

She could hardly believe what he was saying. He was willing to have a real exchange of ideas, listen to what she said. Maybe she could change his mind, convert a detractor into an ally. "If you're going to play Twenty Questions, can I have something to eat? I'm famished."

"All you've done the last few days is eat."

"Must be the fresh air."

"Or the exercise."

She blushed.

"There's some fresh fruit in the backpack."

He didn't exaggerate, she'd learned. "Care for some, Ace?"

"Oh, yeah."

"To eat," she said, with a mock frown.

"Oh, yeah."

"Ace! Be serious."

"I'm trying."

"Try harder."

"I am, darlin', much harder."

She picked up the now-dry shirt he'd discarded. "Mind if I borrow it?"

"Go ahead. It'll look better on you than it ever did on me."

She slipped into the wrinkled garment that had absorbed his masculine scent. She wondered absently if he would notice it missing if she shoved it in with her stuff when she left. Crawling to the end of the sleeping bag, she grabbed the fruit from inside the top of the backpack, then took his pocket knife from a zippered compartment on the side. She sliced a piece of fruit and handed him a section.

"Thanks."

She took a bite from her piece, the juice dribbling down her chin. "This is good."

"Glad you approve."

He finished his portion, then waited.

"Okay," she said, licking her fingers. "Are you sure you want to hear this? It's a long, boring story."

"Bore me."

She crossed her legs, making sure his T-shirt covered her completely, then started, "My company has had some setbacks in recent years."

"Not uncommon."

"You sound like the voice of experience."

"Yeah. Well, it was a long time ago."

She was intrigued. She'd guessed at a depth to Ace he didn't want people to know. And now he'd teased her with it. "Where? When?"

He propped up on both elbows, catching her gaze. He grinned in a way that made her stomach jump. "No dice, darlin'. I asked first."

"I'll tell you if you tell me."

He laughed.

"Is that a 'No way'?"

"As close as they get, Nicky."

He'd made his statement simply, with no malice. And no hint that he'd share any of his past. "I know this certain spot on your—"

"Nicole!"

"I'll tickle you 'til you talk."

"You're welcome to try."

She looked at him speculatively.

"After you answer my questions."

"Since you insist." Nicole folded her arms across her middle. "My father started the firm about twenty years ago. He had a knack for mediation and a knowledge of foreign languages and customs, not to mention a few friends who were ambassadors to various countries.

"And back then, there weren't many competitors in the market. He started WorldNet—"

"Bringing the world together," Ace quoted. "I've seen the ads in magazines."

She nodded. "We were successful, incredibly so, until my father died."

"Go on."

"He started the business with Sam Weeder, my godfather. Sam evidently had other ideas on where the company could expand. My father disagreed." She paused, the pain still like a knife in her heart.

"Sam took a bunch of files and left. He evidently sent letters to our biggest accounts, saying the name of the company had been changed and that there had been a change of corporate address. We haven't been able to prove it, but by all indications, that's what happened."

Ace whistled.

"We were left with small-time clients. And a huge overhead." She raised her hands when he started to say something. "I'm not looking for sympathy, but I just want you to know what's happening. Sam Weeder's firm tried to save this account for my client and failed. WorldNet is their last hope. And they're ours."

"And if you fail?"

Nicole couldn't suppress the shudder that shimmied its way up her spine. She'd tried valiantly—if not successfully—not to think of the repercussions she'd be faced with back in California.

She sucked in a deep breath as Ace's thought replayed in her mind. "I can't fail, Ace. I can't." Nicole closed her eyes for a second, gathering her composure.

"That's a little more pessimistic than I would have expected from you."

"There's nothing pessimistic about it, Ace. We showed a devastating loss last quarter. We can't take that kind of hit again."

He sat up. The sleeping bag covered his hips and legs, but his chest was bare. Late-afternoon shadows filtered through the tent, seemingly lengthening the distance between them.

He raked his hands through hair that had curled after drying.

"A hundred employees will be out of a job if I don't succeed. They have bills and responsibilities. I can't fail them." Nicole felt as though Ace was poised above her, scalpel in hand, forcing her to cut away the layers of protection she'd built around herself. For a reason she didn't even begin to comprehend, Ace wanted to know her innermost secrets. She shuddered when she realized he wouldn't stop short of getting what he wanted. Protectively, she pulled her knees beneath her chin and folded her arms around her shins.

Tears stung her eyes.

"More than that, I can't fail myself."

He waited.

Long minutes dragged between them.

"Nicky?" Somehow he'd tugged on a pair of shorts and was hunched near her. He stroked the curve of her cheekbone while patiently waiting.

Painfully, she faced the reasons she'd buried sometime while she was still in school, when she'd finally figured out the way to win her father's love and approval. "Maybe you don't understand—can't understand—but everything I have, everything I am, is riding on this." She shuddered. "Nothing I have ever done has been good enough. Straight A's weren't enough. Graduating second in my class wasn't good enough. Being accepted to college wasn't enough, because it wasn't the right college.

"I have to succeed, Ace. Because I'm nothing if I fail."

Ten

Ace felt as if he had been slugged in the stomach.

He'd seen Nicole under pressure, seen her hold back tears, frustration, pain. He'd seen her square her shoulders and meet each of his challenges with determination.

He'd felt her response when he held her in his arms, seen the way her body budded beneath his probing touch, his appraisal, his approval.

He'd sensed a vulnerability, though she'd been loath to expose it. That she was driven because of demons didn't surprise him. Most people were. But he hadn't expected her reasons to cut a swath through his heart.

This meant the world to her.

Lord, what had she been through? She shouldn't have to carry the burden alone. Nicole looked at him and he saw anguish in her eyes.

"Come here, darlin'."

He wrapped his arms around her, encouraged her to rest her head on his shoulder. Nicole had obviously missed out on one of the most basic requirements for human happiness: love. He let out his breath. *As if he hadn't.*

Wet tears fell on his chest, but he didn't wipe them away. Nicole needed to purge, and though a saint he wasn't, he intended to be there for her.

Her shoulders shook. Her body trembled. And still he held her, offering the only comfort he knew. Suddenly he wished he knew soft words, words to stop the hurt, words to heal. But he didn't. He'd never heard them.

Though now he wished he had.

He stroked her hair, pleased in a way that was deeply masculine, that she no longer pinned it on top of her head. She left it loose, for him.

Day slipped into night. Sometime before dusk, she'd slept, and he'd held her, shifting so both were nestled in the sleeping bag's comfort.

"I'm sorry," Nicole said softly.

Ace moved, glad she was awake. His arm had cramped, but he'd remained still, not wanting to disturb her. "Don't be."

As if the darkness gave her courage, she admitted, "I've never been in love. I've never had anyone that cared about me more than anything else.

"I was an only child, something of an inconvenience in my father's life, after my mother died. I learned early enough that nothing I did would measure up. Nothing would help Daddy forget the pain of losing my mother."

She fell silent for a second and he didn't push.

"I never got a hug. Not even once." She laughed, but the sound was one of bitterness, not happiness. "I saw other kids get picked up from school. The parents smiled. Sometimes they even hugged their kids."

Her ache was tangible, and he felt it with her.

"Make the hurt go away, Ace." Desperation tinged her tone.

He turned her to face him, stroked back the tears from her face with his thumb, then kissed her in a way he hoped communicated his understanding, the feelings he wanted to share, but didn't know how to voice.

His kiss had tasted of tenderness, she realized as she watched him poke at the fire some time later. She'd asked him to make the hurt go away. He had.

He'd forced her into a confession she thought locked in her soul, and instead of shattering pain, she'd experienced healing.

Ace glanced at her from the other side of the fire. The flickering light lit his eyes with vibrant color. It gave him added intensity.

"You know, Nicky, I like you for who you are. Not for who you pretend to be."

"Pretend?"

"You're a warm, willing woman, and you've hidden it under a tough exterior." He held up his hand when she started to interrupt him. "Wait. Yes, I know you've got guts and stamina—that's not what I'm talking about. I'm talking about toughness, the kind that hides the real you. The real you is sensational, Nicky. Don't forget it."

If she'd had doubts, they were totally erased. She loved Ace Lawson, the first person to ever see beyond her carefully constructed facade. It'd been in place so long, she'd forgotten its existence . . . until Ace toppled it.

But with his ability to see came the ability for him to destroy. He held more ammunition against her than anyone ever had. Because she cared, she was exposed. And that scared her.

Ace offered her a cup of coffee. Black. She grimaced when she took a drink, still unaccustomed to the way he brewed the stuff. "This'll keep me up all night."

"I can always hope."

"I thought I heard you complaining earlier."

"Me? Must be mistaken."

"So what about you, Ace?" She used his own phrase on him. "What's a nice guy like you doing in a place like this?"

"Don't be fooled into thinking I'm a nice guy, Nicole. I'm not."

Nicole wasn't fooled. Despite his contradiction, she knew better. He did things he didn't have to.

"I've been known to be a mean son of a bitch. I've seen the inside of a jail cell—hell, more than one."

And yet she'd seen a tenderness in Ace she doubted most men possessed. The dichotomy fascinated her, and she wondered what had made him the man he was.

"Tell me about it," she encouraged softly.

Implacably, he shook his head.

She sighed. "You said I was welcome to tickle you, to make you talk."

"Won't work," he stated flatly. Ace prodded the tinders that had taken forever to catch hold after the rain. She looked at him and noticed he appeared lost in memories.

She wondered, with a sudden stab of jealousy, if he'd ever been in love. Even married. It didn't matter, she told herself. She and Ace were temporary, to be relegated to the past after he flew her back to L.A. And though she knew she'd fallen for him, he'd given no indication of feeling the same. To him, she was probably just another woman. She tried to pretend that thought didn't chafe. Wanting to know about his past was a form of self-torture. Nevertheless, she did care, because whatever had happened shaped him into the person he was. "Are your parents alive?"

He glanced up. "Don't try to psychoanalyze me, Nicole. It won't work. Professionals can't figure me out. Why should you?"

Softly she said, "Maybe because I care."

For a brief passing of time, she swore the nighttime insects held still. He looked across the dying fire, through the smoke the gentle breeze caused.

"You shouldn't."

She shrugged, a little helplessly. "But I do."

"Don't do this to yourself, Nicole. Don't do it to us."

"It's too late."

He swore, soft and savagely.

She saw him draw a breath deep into his lungs.

"What are you trying to say, Nicole?"

"I'm not *trying* to say anything. I am saying that I care about you. I care about the things that make you unique. You don't scare me, Ace."

"I should."

"You don't. Because no matter what you say or do, there's something inside that's basically good."

"Don't count on it, Nicole. Don't ever count on it."

With that, he went into the tent and zipped the flap shut.

Nicole sighed, then whispered to the forest, "I am, though, Ace. I'm counting on it."

As the night grew on, it became colder. She rubbed her hands up and down her arms, trying to stay warm. Not that it did much good. Her shorts left her legs bare.

Stars emerged, one by one, like the beginning of a magical snowfall. And still she waited, waited for the goodness inside Ace to come through.

She was counting on it.

The light of a nearly full moon trekked overhead. But she didn't doubt. In her heart of hearts, and despite much evidence to the contrary, she still wanted to believe in fairy tales, that good always triumphed over evil.

She lost track of time, stopped trying to count the thousands of stars in the heavens. Instead, she focused on one. The first one that had come out that night, the one she'd wished on . . . even though she was much too much of a realist to think those dreams would translate into a happily-ever-after for a hotshot pilot and corporate career woman.

"Are you coming to bed?"

Her heart flipped.

"Nicky?"

She heard the drag of zipper behind her.

"You'll catch a cold."

"Why would you care?"

"I'm still on your payroll."

"No other reason?"

"No."

Her shoulders sagged. Moments later, she felt his hands on her tired shoulders, massaging, urging, coaxing.

"Nicky?"

"Yes?" she asked, her breath a whisper on the night air.

"Turn around. Face me. Let me look at you."

She did. She tipped her head back so she looked into his face, then held still for a while, letting both their eyesights adjust.

"What do you see in me, Nicky?"

"Want me to be honest, hotshot?"

"Yeah."

"Yeah? In that case..." She trailed off, uncertain if she should push him as far as she was tempted. "I see a liar."

"The last man who called me a liar got a broken jaw." His words were clipped, harsh.

"But I'm a woman."

"I'd noticed."

A chill, nothing to do with the cooling night, lanced up her spine. Had she misread him?

"And you're right," he said a minute later.

The few feet separating them might have been a mile considering the distance she felt from him.

"I lied."

Nicole's heart picked up its tempo. She wanted to go to him, put her arms around him, offer her mouth for his kiss. But she didn't, not knowing how he would respond.

He dragged his fingers through his hair, hair that'd grown longer during the past week. "You're right, Nicky. I do care. Don't ask me why or when the hell it happened, but I do care. You're not just a job. You stopped being a job that night at Poncho and Maria's."

She smiled wanly.

Ace's hand dropped to his side, as though he wasn't sure exactly what to do with it. He crossed to a rock near her, then sat, legs spread wide. His voice, though quiet, carried in the near stillness of the forest. "You were honest with me, I'll try to be honest with you."

His tone was strained. Being open was obviously difficult for him, which made her appreciate his attempt even more. "You asked about my parents. My father's very much alive. As for my mother, I haven't seen her in twenty-some years. She ran off with a Hollywood type who promised her the sun and the moon." He shrugged. "For all I know or care, she's dead."

Nicole winced.

"Dad tried his best, but it's hard for a man to be a mother and father to a hell-raising kid. I got busted a couple times in high school, spent enough time at juvenile detention to decide I didn't want to grow up behind bars. I wanted to fly." He laughed, a scoffing sound. "Anyway, I got this piece of mail from the air force. Officer Training School sounded good so I went to college and got a business degree."

"And then?" she prompted.

"The air force didn't want a screwed-up kid they saw as a potential problem, and I still wanted to fly. I needed money to support my habit, so I took a job as a junior executive at my dad's electronics company, bought a plane and the ground school lessons." With more than a hint of sarcasm, he continued, "Everyone knows a budding executive needs a wife, so I found one."

She tried to ignore the stab of jealousy at the mention of a wife.

"I was still young enough to believe in love when I married Elana. I should have learned from my mother, but I didn't. I was a kid. Idealistic. Stupid. I thought we'd have a couple of babies, you know, grow up with them. I wanted to do all the things with my kids that my dad never did with me. Little League, football—heck, even going to band concerts. Like I said, stupid.''

The hardness she'd come to associate with him was back, in the way he spoke, the way he held his shoulders.

"Elana didn't even want kids, said they'd ruin her figure."

She'd seen Ace with the Maldanados' children. He'd been a natural, patient and teasing. For a second, she tried to picture Ace's kids. Would their eyes have the same odd shade that Ace's did? Would his children be as full of mischief and devilry as Ace himself? And why did the thought of never having kids suddenly make her sad?

"I tried to do things the so-called right way. I worked ten hours a day, six days a week, did the endless circuit of dinner parties and cocktail parties. Within three years, Dad promoted me to an assistant vice president. Old man was proud as hell, thought he'd done okay by his only kid. Only problem was, I hated my job.

"I lived for Sunday afternoons when I'd take my plane up. Then one time I wondered what it would be like if I didn't go back. When I suggested to Elana that there was more to life than new dresses and garden parties with the senator's wife, she suggested I take a hike."

The bitterness made Nicole flinch.

"So I did. She hired a fancy-schmancy lawyer who wiped me out, not that I cared. I wanted out so bad, I'd have given her anything. And I did. Me and Cessie left Dallas a dozen years ago and never looked back."

"No regrets?"

"No regrets."

She knew she and Ace never stood a chance, yet she still felt as though reality was intruding too quickly. "You wouldn't go back to the U.S.?"

"Not a chance. I like my life the way it is."

"No room for changes?"

"None wanted. I fly for a living and I like it. I get more pleasure from the mercy trips I fly than anything I've done in my life. I'm doing something worthwhile, not slitting the other guy's throat before he gets mine, not poring over ledgers when the sun beckons and the night calls. I like running my own business and helping kids as much as I love to fly. I don't get bored. I don't put up with corporate bull. And when I've had enough of a place, I leave."

"Your life is full in every way?"

"Maybe not, but life's a series of choices. I've made mine. I'll live with them."

"And there's nothing that can change your mind?"

"Until a week ago, I didn't think so."

"And now?"

Time missed a beat as they looked at each other. Finally, slowly, he said, "I don't know, Nicky. I don't know."

Dare she hope?

"Come to bed with me?"

She wanted nothing more than to be held by him. The invitation reached all the way to his eyes. She saw the same hopes and fears reflected in his face that she'd seen in her own. She couldn't possibly refuse. "Yes."

He held the tent's flap open. She ducked, brushing by Ace as she went inside. As usual, his nearness affected her with the headiness of fine champagne. His fingers were so light on her behind, she could have imagined the touch, if it weren't for the instant awareness that flooded her body.

Ace followed her inside, sealing the tent, the intimacy. She longed for his touch in a way she couldn't have dreamed possible even a week ago. She suppressed a shudder. How was she going to survive in Los Angeles without him? He was the closest she'd come to feeling love. Ever.

He set a small lantern in one corner of the tent, its light flooding the interior.

"Undress me," she invited.

Carnal passion flared in his eyes. "My pleasure."

His words were spoken at whisper level, yet they torched a frisson of desire that shocked her.

"Shoes and socks first," he said. "Sit down."

She obeyed and in seconds, he'd bared her feet. He fanned his touch across the arch of one foot. She squirmed. He did it again. Her calf muscles tightened in reflex.

"Shorts," he said. "Shouldn't take long."

His cool fingers met her flesh. Awareness made her insides taut. She heard the snap yield, then the teeth of the zipper. Absently, she wondered if he was prolonging the torture intentionally.

Probably. He'd warned her he wasn't a nice guy.

When he'd removed her clothes and his own, she was throbbing. He poised on top of her, then muttered, "Damn."

"What's wrong?"

He rolled off, then sucked in his breath. "Birth control."

"I'll get it."

"Sure?"

"Be right back." They'd slept together. There was no reason for her to be shy. Or so she told herself.

She rooted through the backpack. Her fingers closed around fabric and something that felt like round buttons. She pulled it out. *Pinocchio*. How could she have forgotten? She dropped the briefs with the distended nose, then plunged again to the bottom of the canvas.

Finally she found a few packets. She took one, and asked, "How many more do you have?"

"Don't tell me we'll have to ration them?"

"Looks like it."

"Lord, help me find a drugstore, and quick."

She laughed along with him. "It's all right. We won't be here much longer. How many can you possibly use?"

"With you around? More than what's left—that's for sure."

The thought that their time together was running out bothered her. It meant saying goodbye to Ace, then returning to face an uncertain future. At least she would have memories. . . . The thought didn't cheer her.

Unwilling to let tomorrows ruin today, Nicole responded to the imp inside she usually fought off, the imp Ace awakened. She dug to the bottom of the backpack, in search of the cartoonish briefs.

She went back to Ace, smiling.

"Thanks," he said.

Nicole waited until he'd slipped on the condom, then showed him the briefs.

If possible, her hotshot, macho pilot blushed.

"Wear them for me?"

"Wear them?" he echoed, disbelief edging his voice.

"And then lie to me, Pinocchio. Lie to me."

Eleven

"**D**id you love your wife?"

"Elana?" He considered for a minute. "I thought I did when I married her. About six weeks later, I knew it wouldn't work, but I was stubborn enough to try anyway. Which was a hell of a lot more than she did." Ace tried to contain his bitterness. But still, it was difficult. He didn't like to fail at anything. Yet he had at marriage. Big-time.

The first painted streaks of dawn appeared on the eastern horizon. Neither Nicole nor Ace had slept much. Ace generally hated talking, which he'd realized had been one of the reasons Elana and he hadn't stood a chance. But for some reason, he didn't mind Nicole's questions.

He pulled Nicole closer, enjoying the feel of her hair and her head on his biceps. He could get used to it. Easily.

She was on her side, her stomach pressed against him, thighs curled around his. He inhaled the feminine scent she alone owned and felt an answering response.

"When she refused to listen to my plans for the future, I smelled the coffee, so to speak. Elana wanted to marry a man who was going places. I heard she married a lawyer with political aspirations."

"I'm sorry."

"Don't be. I'm not."

"Tell me about your mercy missions. I read in your files that you fly to Central America frequently with supplies and medicines."

"Your research was top-notch," he said.

"I'm scared to fly, as you know. I wanted to be sure of the person whose hands my fate rested in."

He winced.

"You make monthly flights into poor areas, right?"

He wished he could hire her sleuth. Most people weren't privy to that kind of information about him. "Poor, politically sensitive areas," he agreed. "When I left Elana, I didn't know where I was headed." He looked at her, meeting her gaze with the unflinching directness she'd shown earlier. "You asked about me going to jail."

She nodded expectantly.

"I needed cash, fast, so I took a job I'm not proud of now. It got me shot down and landed my butt in a hostile jail for a couple of months. If it wasn't for Maria Maldanado, I'd probably still be there."

"Maria?"

"Believe it or not, she's trained as an attorney."

"An attorney?"

"Might have been one of the best, except she opted to return to the island after only a year and have a family. Maria still works occasionally, mainly on island stuff. She takes the cases no one else will, and does it gratis."

"Women can have it all these days."

"I'm not saying they can't or shouldn't."

"I'd want it all," Nicole admitted.

"That doesn't surprise me."

"Do you have something against that?"

"Who me? Hell, no, I'm as progressive as the next man. If a woman wants a family and a job, I've got no problem with it. What I've got problems with are women who want everything their way—no exceptions, no flexibility." He should have seen Elana's single-minded determination to be nothing other than an executive's wife. In retrospect, he realized he needed a woman by his side who would help rather than hinder, a woman as capable and gutsy as himself.

A woman like Nicole.

He shoved the thought aside with a speed bordering on brutality. In her own way, Nicole was as determined as Elana.

And yet . . .

Nicole had said she wanted kids. A home and a career. And she'd proven herself worthy. She was the type of person he wanted, needed with him in Risky Business. He hated the business end of things, even though he was good at it. Secretaries came and went, none of them having what it took to stay in the ramshackle building with no running water, haphazard electricity and occasional telephone service. But it hadn't really surprised him. Not many of the women he'd hired had known what a typewriter was. And since most of his business was done for American companies needing special skills, his employees' lack of English as a second language was a hindrance.

If he had a partner, someone as dedicated to the firm as he, no doubt he could turn Risky Business into a profitable business.

It'd been a lot of years since someone had actually been around to notice whether or not he made it back at night. Not that his room in the back of Risky's shack was a real home. Still, to have someone who gave a damn whether or not he crashed...

What the hell. He'd made his choices. He lived with them. He made enough on the few missions he did fly to pay for fuel and medical supplies. What more could he ask?

"You know, I've always admired men like you, Ace. Men who venture where others don't dare tread. You're a rare breed."

"I'm no John Wayne, Nicky."

"No. You're much better."

"I do what I do because I want to. Pure and simple."

"That doesn't make it less noble."

Her breath was warm on him. Intoxicating. Like a drowning man to a lifeline, he couldn't seem to get enough. "Maybe not."

"So why do you do it?"

"Are you gonna hang a 'psychiatrist' shingle on your office door when you get back?"

"There probably won't be an office door when I get back," she said. Her sigh of regret slashed deeply into him. "I'm just curious."

"Ah. I see. I guess I've never really taken the time to analyze it. I do it because it feels good, I guess."

"Why did you do it the first time?"

The pain of that memory still ached. "I was flying ammo to rebels."

"Isn't that illegal?"

"Only if you get caught." Her hand that had been making slow circles on his chest froze. He'd warned her he wasn't all good. There were parts of him that were nasty, parts he would rather forget, but they were every bit as much a part of him as the good things. He just hoped when he died that the good outweighed the bad and that he'd earn wings of another kind. They wouldn't feel like Cessie, but he wouldn't be earthbound, or worse.

Her hand began to move again and he expelled his breath. "Anyway, when I landed, this kid—Miguel— I'll never forget him—came up to the plane. He was eight or nine, but full of mischief. Just like me. He climbed in the plane while I was unloading it, then conned me into taking him for a ride. He said he wanted to be a pilot when he grew up." Ace's fist tightened at his side. "Damnedest thing was, he never got the chance to grow up. Next time I went to his village, he was dead. Measles, if you can believe it. In this day and age a kid died from the measles."

His arm tightened around Nicole, as if she could help the pain go away. She did. "I didn't want any other kids to die."

"I'm sorry."

"Yeah. So was I." While they'd talked, the sun had made progress. They'd lost a couple hours of daylight already, and would lose more if they stayed in bed any longer. "We've got to go, Nicky."

"Now?"

"We're meeting Poncho tomorrow."

She helped pack, though he sensed a reluctance on her part to leave. He echoed it. They ate a quick breakfast, then rubbed bug repellent into each other's exposed skin—and she had quite a bit of it, he noted with masculine appreciation. What she did for a pair of shorts should have been illegal. Probably was in some parts of the world.

"Ready to go?"

She nodded, then they started back. Ace knew it would take two days less to return to civilization than it had taken to reach the lake, since he would take the direct route.

Nicole kept silent, and he looked behind him periodically to make sure she was still with him. She hadn't been so quiet since the beginning of the trip. But the silence suited him. He didn't feel like talking. Though the heat was oppressive, Nicole had left her hair loose. It teased her shoulders, and his memory.

For the first time, the idea of going back into the sky alone didn't seem appealing. Hell, the heat was affecting his brain. Definitely a short circuit. Definitely.

Later that afternoon he stopped and unscrewed the lid to the canteen. He offered it to Nicole, then took a swig.

"There's something I've been meaning to talk to you about," he said, putting the lid back on, then wiping the back of his hand across his sweat-dampened brow.

Caution, mixed with another emotion he couldn't name, jumped into her eyes. "Yes?"

"The plant." He saw her back stiffen, and it was as if all the passion they'd shared suddenly vanished. "If we get back and the democratic government is restored to power, I want you to withdraw your company's name as the mediator."

"How can you ask that of me after all we've shared?"

Her voice had risen several octaves. She couldn't have sounded more shocked if he asked her to have a date with the devil. "I'm asking *because* of what we shared, Nicky. You've seen things from a different perspective. I was hoping—"

"You hoped wrong, Ace. Are you trying to tell me you slept with me only to get me to change my mind?"

"You can't actually believe that."

"What else can I believe? Was it all a game to you?"

"I guarantee you, darlin', the last thing this is is a game. This is real, this is life."

"I'm sorry," she said, her voice softly hoarse. "I can't."

The stark pain etched across her eyes almost made him drop the issue. Almost. But too much was riding on the outcome for him to relent. He had to seize his last opportunity. "You spent the night at the Maldanados'. Did they seem poor to you?"

"They didn't have indoor plumbing."

"So quality of life depends on having three toilets in three different bathrooms, all of them that flush seven gallons of water at a time?"

"To a large extent, yes."

"You're a snob, Nicky. Through and through. I thought you were different." The words were calculated for effect. They scored. And hurt him, too. Damn. "Did you enjoy the last few days?"

"Until about five minutes ago."

"We didn't have running water."

"That's different."

"Is it? Why?"

"Because we were camping, not living."

"Did the Maldanados' kids look like they were suffering? Even though they don't have indoor plumbing?"

She shoved her hair over her shoulders. "What's your point?"

He held her by the upper arms. He wondered if she felt the same current that passed through him when their flesh joined. "My point is, the Maldanados are happy with their lives. They may be poor by penthouse apartment standards, but they have a richness I envy. They're happy."

"They'd be a lot happier if they had more money."

"They have everything they need. So do all the islanders. Their standard of living may not be high—certainly not what you might even consider livable—but they have everything they need.

"Almost everyone here works. Everyone has a place in a storm. Everyone has something to eat before they go to bed at night. Tell me one other place that can make that claim."

"What about the rebels?"

"Islanders who refuse to change their ways. No—" he held up a hand "—I don't sanction what they did, nor their motivation, but I do understand it. Until Rodriguez and his progressive ideas found power, there were no rebels on Cabo de Bello. Once they think they've won, I doubt we'll hear from them again. So far, no innocent people have been harmed. Yes, there have been a few incidents, but they were definitely political in nature."

She shook her head, feeling deflated and defeated, but still unwilling to give up. "I can't stop now, Ace. You've got to understand what's on the line for me, for my company, for my client. We'll bring jobs for the rest of the people.''

"But not good jobs." His fingers dug into her flesh.

"I'm sorry, Ace. Please, please try to see my point."

"Hell, Nicky. I thought I'd gotten to know you better than that."

"You're hurting me."

Instantly he released her. He saw her drag a gulp of air into her lungs.

"If the rebels have been overthrown, I have a job to do, with or without your approval."

"Remember one thing, darlin', WorldNet can't keep you warm at night. Maybe it can give you a sense of satisfaction, but it won't kiss you and it won't pat you on the back when you do something wonderful. It won't laugh with you or smile at you. It can't be your lover. Think about it." Ace grabbed the backpack from the ground, then offered a quick prayer that the rebels still retained power. It was his only hope...Cabo de Bello's only hope.

That night, Nicole forced herself to sleep as far away from him as the sleeping bag would allow. She curled into a self-protective ball, a position that was common at home, but unfamiliar over the past few days. She'd learned to like snuggling next to Ace's body. But tonight was different. They'd hardly spoken a word the rest of the day. His gibes had hurt badly. In exposing her innermost fears, she'd laid open her heart and become vulnerable. And he'd used it all against her. Like the jerk he'd claimed to be.

She should have believed him, but she hadn't. She'd seen an underlying tenderness, but had been stupid to believe he'd let it rule him.

Ace shifted, and against her buttocks she felt that he was hard. Regret washed through her. The past few days had been some of the most emotionally enriching of her life. Under his guidance, she'd blossomed sexually. She should hate him for destroying the memories. But she was incapable of it. He'd insinuated himself into her heart, and she knew he was going to stay. Every time she'd see a light aircraft, she would think of him. And remember. She only hoped she could convince her heart to store the good and not the bad.

She slept fitfully, trying to keep still so she didn't arouse Ace and succumb to his smoldering sensuality again. The only way to survive the coming ordeal the next day was to harden her heart. As if it were possible.

"Change your mind yet?"

She wondered how long he'd been awake, wondered if he was as aware of her as she was of him. "No."

"Are you at least thinking?"

"No. My mind's made up."

"Yeah. It would be."

Without any apparent sense of embarrassment, he climbed out of the sleeping bag, then pulled on his jeans, leaving the material loose. He was so tempting. So dangerous.

"Getting up, or would you like me to join you?"

She sat up to his mocking laughter.

"If I didn't know better, I'd think you were a coward."

For a brief second, she wished for the intimacy they'd shared. She banished the thought as quickly as it came. Yesterday was over, she told herself. And tomorrow looked to be a bigger challenge.

He left the tent and she dressed quickly. She'd been wishing their trip could be prolonged. Now she was grateful it ended today. One way or another. By nightfall, she would know whether she could pull it off. Or lose it all.

Within thirty minutes, before the sun became hot, they left their campsite and headed back to civilization.

The distance between her and Ace couldn't be bridged with words, she realized. It would take a total change of attitude. She wouldn't change hers. And as surely as the next corporate takeover, he wouldn't change his.

They exchanged only a couple of sentences during lunch, and none when they took a break several hours later. She missed him. Even though he was never more than five yards away, she missed him—his smile, his tease, his touch.

She wondered how she'd manage by herself when the lonely night stretched in front of her. Now that she'd known tenderness, she could miss it.

WorldNet can't keep you warm at night.... It can't be your lover. She heard Ace's words as surely as though he'd spoken them now. Then she remembered something else he'd said. Life was a series of choices. For better or worse she'd made hers. *Regret* wasn't part of her vocabulary.

The ache inside had taken root in her heart by the time dusk descended. Not more than ten minutes later, they emerged from the trees, and saw Poncho's taxi parked on the far side of the unpaved road. Her feet hurt, she couldn't catch her breath and her shoulders burned.

She was a wreck.

And, once again, Ace was the reason.

Ace strode across the road and knocked on the car's windshield.

"Where's the *señorita?* You leave her in the forest, no?"

"It was tempting." Ace turned to her. "Your chariot awaits."

Nicole crossed the road, then took hold of the taxi's door handle. She swung the door wide, catching Ace's shin. "You know what they say about being led into temptation. You might get burned."

He swore. "Or win the door prize." With another curse in a language she didn't recognize, he slid in beside her.

Poncho ground the transmission into gear, and Nicole coughed at the dirt that came through the floor. At least some things didn't change. The man lost the car's rear end on a curve and she noticed Ace wince when his injured shin banged the back of the driver's seat. Served him right.

"*¿Que pasa, mi amigo?*" Ace asked.

"Señor Mendino, he is governor now."

Ace nodded.

"The leader of the Peoples Progressive Party?" Nicole asked.

She thought Ace wasn't going to answer. Then he turned to her. "You've done your homework."

Though she tried not to let it, his sarcasm stung. "He's not as progressive as Rodriguez."

"Which is probably why he's still alive."

Her stomach churned. She'd thought all of her problems would be over if the rebels were out of power. She hadn't considered the possibility that the newly appointed leader might not be receptive to her mediation.

Ace's shoulder brushed against hers as the car swayed. She was so aware of him, more so now since they'd shared the most intimate of human sensuality.

"Is it safe for us to refuel?"

"*Sí.*"

Nicole grabbed Ace by the arm. "We can't leave, not yet. I need to talk to Mendino."

"I wouldn't think of hurting your career, darlin'. Don't worry. We don't fly until you give the word."

He instructed Poncho to drive to the governor's mansion.

Nicole tried to relax against the seat, but found it difficult, and not because the vinyl was cracked and peeling. Almost too soon, Poncho turned onto a smoothly oiled road. After days in the wilderness, the idea of meeting the governor felt overwhelming. She wanted a shower, needed to clean up.

A gate in the distance was closed and a guard stood on duty. Full circle, she realized. Only this time, the guard didn't look as threatening.

Beside her, Ace appeared relaxed. His body held no tension as he rolled down the window.

"Nicole Jackson of WorldNet to see the governor."

The man leaned forward, looking at Nicole.

"Señorita Jackson has been expected for some time," the guard said.

"*Sí,*" Ace agreed. "We were unavoidably detained."

"Perhaps for the better." The man nodded, then signaled another guard inside a wooden shack to open the gate. After saluting, he waved them through.

The taxi's headlight lit the way, and as far as Nicole could see, there was no evidence of the brutality that had taken place in the last week.

"Looks can be deceiving," Ace said, as though he'd read her mind.

"Yeah," she agreed, her language lacking the formality she always used at home. "So I'm learning."

She couldn't read his expression in the dark, but sensed he knew she wasn't referring only to the island's politics.

Poncho stopped and Ace climbed out, offering Nicole his hand.

He didn't hold on to her any longer than necessary. She felt a tug of regret for what they'd shared, for what was now nothing but a part of the past. And it hurt worse to know that she could bridge the breach with a few words. Words she wasn't able to speak.

Ace and Nicole climbed the stairs together, her heart pounding with each step. Emotions she couldn't begin to sort out gushed through her.

Her hand shook. She didn't know what she did want from what she didn't want. And the next few minutes would seal her future, whether she would save the account and give her company money to survive the quarter, or whether she would see her dreams crumble to dust at her feet. But she had the truly frightening feeling that regardless of what happened, she wouldn't see Ace again.

She wondered why it hurt so much.

The door was opened by a young man who showed Ace and her into a small, elegantly furnished room off the side of the foyer. When the man's footsteps faded in the distance, she looked at Ace.

His face was set, jaw squared. The growth of beard shadowing his face lent him a dark, dangerous air that made her nervous. It was difficult to believe this was the same man who teased her, made love to her. Never had she felt so far apart from him. And never had she needed his strength more than she did right now.

A knot formed in her throat. It wasn't like her to be so emotional. In her family, tears were a sign of weakness, better hidden so no one used your vulnerability against you.

"It doesn't have to be this way, Nicky."

Her name sounded like a caress on his lips. He reached out, placing his hands on her shoulders. She couldn't have moved if she wanted to. She was desperate to make him understand, shake his resolve, yet words weren't adequate.

She swiped away a stray tear, aching inside in a way she hadn't dreamed possible. She recalled an old saying about better to have loved and lost than to have never loved. The saying was wrong. Life would have been easier if she hadn't experienced the depth of emotion she had for Ace.

"Give it up, Nicky. Please. For us."

"I can't. Why can't you see that's not possible for me? I've worked all my life to get where I've gotten—"

"Which is where? What have you done that's productive? Name an achievement that you can be proud of, that's going to last even after you're dead. What's the inscription going to read on your epitaph? Beloved what? Wife? No. Mother? No."

"A woman doesn't need to be a wife and a mother to be successful."

"That's true," he agreed. With more gentleness, he asked, "So what's it going to say, Nicky? Anything you're going to be proud of when you look back on your life?"

She tilted her head to look at him. "I can be proud of the fact I fought for what I believed in. I tried to save my company and give my employees a chance at a good living.''

He stroked a thumb along her cheekbone with infinite tenderness, a motion that warred with the stormy warning on his face. ''I didn't want it to come to this.''

''But it did.'' It was as though he'd ripped out her heart and exposed its flaws.

''I've never said these words before, not to anybody. You're different, Nicole. I tried not to let you, but you worked your way into my heart.''

Her eyes stung with unshed tears. She blinked, then realized the act spilled the emotion she was trying to hide.

''I fell in love with you, Nicky.''

She trembled. Words she longed to hear. But they came too late. Way too late. And she swore her heart would bleed.

''I don't have any alternatives,'' she said desperately. ''I couldn't live with myself if I give up, failing the people depending on me.''

''Darlin', life's a series of choices. Make the right one for a change. Take an empty-handed leap of faith. You won't be disappointed.''

''How can you make that promise?''

His touch felt infinitely tender. ''Take a chance, Nicky. Gamble a little.''

She heard footsteps growing louder.

''Look, Nicky, think about it. You told me once you cared about me.''

''Not enough to let you manipulate me.''

''I'm not trying to—''

''You are.''

He shook his head. ''Convince you, maybe. Manipulate, no.''

Voices blended together outside the door. Ace's fingertips dug into her arms, but she didn't feel pain, only a desperation that things not end this way.

"Take a chance, Nicky. Forget L.A. Come with me."

"What?" Even in her imagination, she hadn't anticipated he'd ask her to go with him. It was a dream come true.

An impossibility.

"I need you. I want you. Come with me, help me."

"Ah, Señorita Jackson, I've been expecting you."

She broke eye contact with Ace reluctantly. There was so much more to be said, and no time to say it. She felt as though a bomb were ticking inside, about to explode.

"I'm very pleased to meet you."

She shook Eduardo Mendino's hand.

"You were to arrive a week ago, no?"

"We were delayed," Ace supplied smoothly.

"Ah, perhaps it is for the best, no? We had a little . . . how would you say—" he waved a hand "—incident last week."

"I'd heard," Ace said dryly.

"And you are?"

"Lawson. Ace Lawson. The lady's pilot."

"I've heard of you. You, too, are welcome, *señor.*" The man turned again to Nicole. "Nevertheless, I'm delighted to meet you, *señorita.* I'm sure you'll enjoy your stay."

She smiled, a false smile that betrayed none of her inner turmoil. And she had a lot of that.

"Señor Rodriguez told me about your plans for opening the plant. I feel it only fair to warn you, *señorita,* Señor Rodriguez and I differed in our opinions."

"Yes, I understand that."

"And yet you are still here."

Nicole squared her shoulders, knowing what she said next would be a slap in the face to Ace. "I'd like to try and change your mind."

"Well, of course, Señorita Jackson."

"This sounds like a personal conversation."

The sarcasm in Ace's tone cut through her heart. She bit her bottom lip not to cry out. She looked at him, seeing defeat settle on his face. She didn't know what to say. There was nothing to say. And everything to say.

The door clicked closed behind him. He'd disappeared.

Along with her hopes of love.

Twelve

—————

Nicole woke, the warm Caribbean breeze drifting through the partially opened window. She moved her toes, then her legs, then finally her fingers and arms. She was still alive, even though she didn't feel like it.

When Ace walked out, it had taken all her self-control not to run after him, beg him to stay, promise the world, swear she'd go along with what he wanted, if only he'd hold her again.

But like he'd said, life was a series of choices. She'd made hers. And would have to live with the consequences, and worse, the regrets.

Last night, the governor had offered her a room upstairs, complete with running water. She'd stripped, taken a hot bath, letting the steam swirl around her, allowing the water to ease the aches in her muscles, the tension in her shoulders.

But it hadn't worked. All she'd thought about was Ace. She remembered the feel of his fingers on her knotted back, the sensations as he manipulated tired limbs. She remembered the taste of his lips, the scent of him as he approached her with a devilish gleam in his eyes.

She remembered the wanting, waiting. The anticipation. The culmination.

She sat up, dragging the cotton sheet around her. Hastily she dressed, but certainly not for success. The clothes were far too wrinkled for that.

Finishing getting ready to meet Señor Mendino took little time, since she had no makeup or curling iron. She was tempted to pull her hair into a ponytail, but frowned when she realized she didn't have a holder.

Nicole dropped onto the edge of the bed. Even if she had an entire makeup case at her disposal, it wouldn't have helped. She hadn't slept all night and no amount of cosmetics could hide the fact.

Though she'd tried not to let them, Ace's words haunted her, replaying in her mind until she was sick of hearing the echo of truth.

The ache in her heart told her, with blinding certainty, that the loss of everything she'd worked for would hurt less than the loss of love.

Nicole stood and crossed the bare, hardwood floor to the window. The second-story room had a view of the coast. Gentle waves rolled against white sand, as if the future didn't depend on what happened in this mansion.

She leaned her forehead on the warm glass and stared into the distance. Kids ran toward the ocean, diving in with the exuberance of youth. She smiled. Many times she'd wanted to do the same thing, but her father didn't swim. So, during the few times they'd vacationed,

Nicole had dutifully sat on the beach. Another good memory that never got made.

I fell in love with you.

She heard Ace's words as clearly as if he stood behind her, whispering them in her ear. She closed her eyes and massaged the lids, hoping to ease some of the burning sensations.

Pictures clouded her mind. She felt ripped in two. She had a job to do, a company to save. But Ace had shown her another point of view.

But she was caught between the proverbial rock and hard place. She didn't want to destroy a way of life for islanders, couldn't destroy her own company.

Yet she realized now that Ace was right about the sweatshop conditions. She'd let her lust for success interfere with her sense of right and wrong.

A silent tear slipped down her face and trickled over her chin.

Going into the small bathroom, she splashed cool water on her face, catching her reflection in the mirror. The sight shocked her. Eyes were bloodshot, nose red, expression haunted. And she didn't like what she saw.

Ace was right. Life was a series of choices. Maybe she had to make some difficult ones. With determination, she squared her shoulders. Only through losing did she know she could win and erase the pain in her eyes.

Determinedly, she unlatched her briefcase Poncho had remembered to bring, taking out the laptop computer. Firing it up, she simultaneously reached for the phone and resolutely punched in Sam Weeder's home phone number.

The sun blindsided him like the Concorde at supersonic speed.

Ace winced, put his hands on his temples, then groaned.

"Always a fool, Ace?"

He pried open one eyelid. "Maria." His eyelid fell closed again. "Hell."

"Good morning to you, too."

"Go away, Maria."

She laughed and the sound scratched across his mind. "Tequila?"

He groped on the floor beside him, then picked up an empty bottle and stared at it, trying to make out the letters that blurred together. "Mescal."

"Did it help?"—

Lord, the woman was worse than Nicole.

"I didn't think so," Maria said, dragging a chair across the floor so that she sat across from him. "Where is she?"

He didn't pretend to be stupid. Maria wasn't. "The governor's mansion."

Maria smiled. "I doubt she can change Eduardo's mind."

"Yeah, me, too."

"So why the booze?"

"Don't you have kids to take care of?"

"Some are playing, others left for school hours ago."

"What the hell time is it?"

"Ten."

He groaned again. He hadn't slept, he'd passed out. "Coffee?"

He sat up, then frowned when every muscle protested. "Thanks." She handed him a cup. Black and strong.

Maria waited, albeit impatiently, for him to finish before bombarding him again. "You fell in love with her, didn't you?"

He stared at the few grounds at the bottom of the cup.

"You're a fool," she said gently.

He nodded, then winced. The coffee worked its magic, breathing life back into his body. "Where's your husband?"

"He was sick, then went to help Ricardo at the airstrip."

"Never could hold his liquor."

"Not true, *amigo*. You just have superhuman abilities."

"Not when it comes to women, apparently." He slid the cup onto a table. He loved Nicole, with a passion that obliterated everything else. Not even the dulling numbness of booze could help him forget that. And as dawn had taken over the black sky, he wished he hadn't been so pigheaded.

He should have said sweet words, instead of being a bully. Why had he pushed her? Nicole Jackson wasn't a woman to push around. He knew that.

"Want to talk about it?" Maria asked.

"No."

"A piece of advice then, from an old friend?"

"I think you're going to give it, whether I want to hear it or not."

"Life's short Ace. Just because Elana was only out for herself, doesn't mean Nicole is."

"Even you don't approve of her politics."

"That doesn't change who she is inside." She placed a hand on his shoulder. "If we were all as judgmental as you, Ace, where would we be? Look ahead, not behind. After some of the things you've done, I'm surprised you're throwing the first stone."

Maria left, after placing a bottle of aspirin and a glass of water on the table. Ace swallowed a couple of the white tablets, then forced himself to stand. He felt like hell.

He wiped a hand down his face. The stubble had become a beard. He needed a shave and a shower.

He needed Nicole.

Ace cursed his stupidity. He'd accused Nicole of being unwilling to compromise, while he'd never been exactly great at the art, either. Hell, since he'd opened Risky Business, everything had been his way. Or no way. He was his own boss, set his own hours, took only the jobs he wanted to.

He thought about the fullness of the week he'd shared with Nicole. In contrast, the past few years of his life had been nothing but a shell. And he'd blown the chance to explore things with Nicole with his ultimatums.

Maria was right. He was a fool.

Ace strode to his backpack, rooted through it for a clean shirt and came up with Pinocchio.

He remembered Nicole's blush when she'd asked him to wear the underwear. She'd smiled tantalizingly that night as she responded to his touch.

Ace took out a shirt, then pulled it over his chest. He thought, long and hard about Nicole. She'd made him feel again, worked her way into his life and mended his heart.

He realized he'd need to compromise, make some changes if he wanted a real shot at love, at the real thing. He hated being tied to the ground, but if that's what it took, he was willing to try. Having Nicole in his arms when dawn stained across inky skies was worth it.

The potential for good outweighed the potential for bad, he was convinced.

He hoped it wasn't too late to save his soul.

Grabbing his backpack, Ace headed for the door.

"Will you be back?"

He stopped, then dropped a kiss on Maria's forehead. "I don't know."

Maria only smiled.

It wasn't far to the governor's mansion and he relished the physical exercise. Maybe the exertion would exorcise some of the demons driving him.

An hour later he arrived at the gate. The guard informed Ace that Nicole was down at the ocean.

The walk hadn't helped. He was still wound tighter than a single-engine plane at thirteen-thousand feet.

His feet sank in the sand. She must have sensed his presence, because she looked up when he approached.

She'd been crying.

Her cheeks were stained, her nose rubbed red. The wind whipped her hair around her, strands sticking to her face.

His pace slowed as he approached her. Now that he was here, he didn't know what to say, how to act. He who'd never lacked for a word was suddenly tongue-tied, even though he'd rehearsed a hundred different approaches during the hike.

Her hand shook as she reached to smooth the hair from her face. "Congratulations," she said. "You won."

He saw her square her shoulders. "What?"

"There'll be no opening."

He felt no triumph, sharing in her defeat. "I'm sorry."

"Don't be. I lost, but my company didn't."

He quirked a brow.

"I called Sam Weeder."

His heart contracted.

Her lower lip trembled. "I negotiated to sell to him."

"Oh, God, babe."

"My attorneys worked on it all morning. Weeder's keeping all my employees and took back the account. He has some alternative plans for a small town in Mexico that's anxious for American development. He has the resources WorldNet didn't. The client has a setback, but not permanent. And my employees are all guaranteed work."

He reached for her, raw, carnal thoughts clawing at him. She surrendered to his embrace, and Ace had never felt as whole and healed as he did right then.

Nicole looked up at him. Hunger and vulnerability were etched in her features. He felt as though he'd been nailed with a sledgehammer.

"You came for me."

"Yeah," he said gruffly. "I came for you. I decided you are worth anything, even flying through fire." He paused, trying to find the courage she'd shown in laying open her heart at his feet. He gulped. Twice. "Will you have me, Nicole?"

She swallowed deeply. "I know I've been all the things you've accused me of being, but I love you, Ace. I know I'm not perfect, and I can't promise I can change, but—"

"Just say you'll take a chance with me?"

Nicole nodded.

"Nicky, are you sure? I don't have a house. I have a shack, with no running water. Risky Business's office has spiders. It's not what you're accustomed to. It—"

"It has you, right?"

"But is it enough?"

"It's enough, Ace. I'll take my chances with you, if you'll let me." She met his gaze, passion shining through the sheen of tears. "I love you. And you love me for who I really am. What more could I possibly ask?"

She stood on her toes and offered him her mouth.
"Nicky..."
"Kiss me, Ace, please."
With a feeling he'd never experienced surging through his loins, he leaned down and captured her mouth. Her kiss was warm, willing, inviting. Just like the woman herself.

She melded against him, and he swept her into his arms.

"Where are we going?"
"To find a place to pitch the damn tent before I take you right here in the open."
Her laughter filled his ears. And thoughts of their future filled his mind.

"Do you have any more of them foil packages left?"
He swore. The longing in his loins was painful.
"What if you don't need one?"
"Don't need one?" He released her, stepping back slightly so he could see the expression on her face.

"I'd like to have a baby, Ace. Your baby."
God, the words were sweet, a dream fulfilled. An opportunity to erase the past. He'd be a good father, and he knew Nicky would be an excellent mother. They'd both have it all. Triumphantly, he swung her into his arms again. "Hot damn!"

Epilogue

Nicole pushed a wisp of hair back from her face and blew air up, trying to dry the sweat dotting her forehead. It had been unbelievably hot the past few days, though the thermometer didn't show it.

She struggled to her swollen feet, hampered by the size of her belly. The baby gave a vicious kick at being disturbed. "Settle down, sweetheart," Nicole crooned as she gently rubbed her stomach in smooth, arcing caresses. "It won't be much longer."

"Sweetheart" kicked again. Nicole's lips twisted, and she couldn't decide whether to grin or grimace. The child was going to have the devil's own—Ace's—temper. The doctor had already confirmed the baby was a boy. She wondered how she would cope with two of them.

A pain squeezed at the base of her spine. She would find out how she would cope within the next few weeks.

Above, the Casablanca fan gave a pathetic wheeze, then wound to a slow stop.

She was starting to climb on the table to fix the fan when Ace strode through the door.

"What the hell do you think you're doing, Mrs. Lawson?"

She stopped. "Fixing the fan."

"Get down."

"You're still bossy, hotshot."

She heard his footfall on the wooden floor.

"And you're still stubborn."

It wasn't easy, but he wrapped his arms around her to lift her down from the chair.

"You're going to hurt yourself," she said, even as she snuggled into him.

"And you're not?" He quirked an eyebrow.

"I was being careful. I do have excellent balance."

"Did, darlin', did."

"Is that another reference to my waistline?"

"'Fraid so." With an exaggerated "oomph," he set her down. "How are you feeling?"

"Fat."

"You don't look fat."

She reached up and placed a kiss on his cheek. "Now I remember why I married you."

Ace reached up and fiddled with the fan. Within seconds, the temperamental blades began to churn through the humid air. "Better?"

"Much. Thanks."

"You hungry? Need something to drink?"

"I'm pregnant, not helpless."

"Humor me."

She gladly accepted the glass of lemonade he poured with a grateful smile. "It's hot."

"Eighty degrees is warm, not hot."

"Not when you're carrying another person inside."

"I'll take your word for it." He sat on the rocking chair he'd bought for her and the baby, then pulled Nicole onto his lap. "Have I told you today how much I love you?"

"You can tell me again if you want." She didn't get tired of hearing the words. She hadn't thought it possible but she loved her husband now more than she had a year ago.

They'd grown together, made choices together, made life together. And she couldn't have been happier.

"I love you, Nicky Lawson."

"I love you, Ace."

They'd both learned the art of compromise. Ace no longer flew dangerous missions, leaving that to the three maverick pilots he'd hired two months after their marriage. Ace flew his mercy missions, but returned as quickly as possible to their newly built headquarters/condo in Belize . . . a condo with running water and a toilet that flushed.

With the money she'd invested over the course of her career, they were able to live comfortably. Running Risky Business satisfied her career ambitions, and she'd parlayed his small operating revenue into bigger returns. The people they helped appreciated it.

"Did he just kick me?" Ace asked when his hand, which had been resting on her stomach, moved.

She winced. "He thinks he's ready to fly."

"How about his mother?"

"More than ready." After a few more restless minutes, the baby settled again.

"I wanted to let you know Cruz is going to pick up the slack for the next few weeks. I'm not going out again until after you have our baby."

She was touched. "That's not necessary. I've got Blanca close by, in case of an emergency."

"Lady, I intend to be here when our son is born. I want to be the one holding your hand."

"And you say I'm stubborn?"

"Bossy, too."

He nuzzled close to her, the feel of his breath on her neck exciting all the feelings she'd always had for him.

"What did Doc say about making love with your husband?"

A slow smile spread across her face. "He told me to make sure I get a back rub, first."

"Ah, the price a man must pay."

He kissed her with an intensity that made her stomach flutter. And the baby stir.

"It's tough," she agreed. "But someone's gotta do it."

"You feel up to it?"

"Does it rain in the tropics?"

"Is that a yes?"

"That's a yes," she answered him.

"No regrets?"

"I love you," she said with feeling. "No regrets."

*   *   *   *   *

Four talented authors make their Silhouette debut—
and you are invited to join the celebration.
Don't miss any of these exciting titles:

HONEYMOON SUITE
(Romance #1113) by Linda Lewis

A prim-and-proper lady must find her way into a confirmed
bachelor's bedroom—any way she can.

THE ROGUE AND THE RICH GIRL
(Desire #960) by Christine Pacheco

After setting out to seduce a serious-minded lady, a sexy
rogue discovers how hot a plain Jane can be.

AND FATHER MAKES THREE
(Special Edition #990) by Laurie Campbell

One single mom and one rebellious teenager meet the man
who just might make their family complete.

ONE FORGOTTEN NIGHT
(Intimate Moments #672) by Suzanne Sanders

With no memory of her past, a woman suspected of a crime
must trust a handsome detective to clear her name—and give
her a future.

PREMIERE: The stars of tomorrow—making their
debut today!

Only from Silhouette®